Mr Lucky

Trentbridge Crime Series
Book One

Lee Wood

Rollercoaster Publishing

Mr Lucky

Copyright

First published by Sound Publishing in 2019.
This edition was published by Rollercoaster Publishing 2023.

Paperback ISBN: 978-1-871407-37-2
Large Print Edition: 978-1-871407-62-4

Mr Lucky

Lee Wood

BRITISH CRIME WRITER

Map of Trentbridge

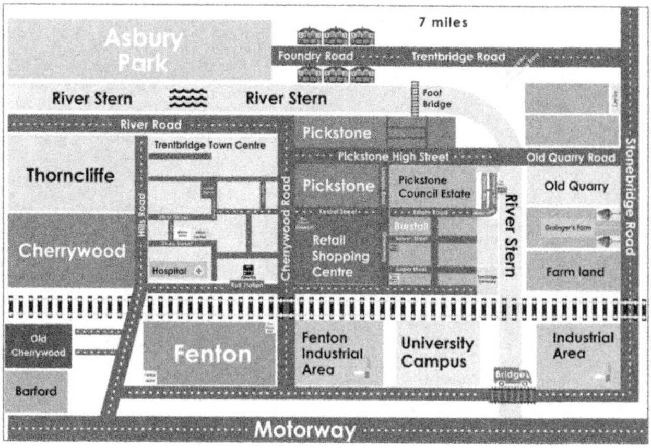

A town based in the North West of England, with a population of 260,000

CHAPTER ONE

HARRY RICHARDSON

There was no doubting the strength of Samson Isaacks. Six feet six tall, with muscles bigger than most men's arms. Currently, he was holding Roger Packman, better known by his acting name Marcus King, upside down out of the top floor window of a six-storey building with one of Samson's fists around the man's ankle as the only means of support. Whilst, at the same time, eating an apple with his other hand.

His boss, Harry Richardson, was standing nearby shouting at the upside-down man.

"Did you think you could steal from me and get away with it? I'm going to spin a coin. Heads, Samson pulls you in and beats the shit out of you. Tails, he lets go of your leg."

The man outside the window was panicking. "I'm sorry," he sniffled. "I didn't mean to."

"Oh, you're sorry. That's all right then. What do you think, Samson? Should we drop the bastard?"

Samson took another bite of his apple and looked at Richardson. "Yeah, good idea, boss. My arm's beginning to ache a bit."

"No, no, please!" screamed the upside-down figure.

"Okay, Samson, bring him in and let's teach him a lesson."

The strongman lifted the hapless wimp back through the window, making sure to smack his head on the window sill. Then he let go and allowed him to freefall two feet onto the hard floor.

Harry Richardson took a step forward and leaned in towards the snivelling man.

"You stole my property. Those drugs were mine, not yours. I paid you well to deliver them, and this is how you repay me. Tell you what I'm going to do. What you stole was worth five grand. That lovely Audi you've got sitting outside must be worth, what, fifteen. How about we do an exchange? You sign the car over to me, and in return, you walk away with your legs not broken. How does that sound?"

"But I need–"

"Samson..."

"No, wait. Take the car."

"Where's the log book and registration?"

"In the glove compartment."

Harry held out his hand. "Keys."

Roger pulled the keyring from his pocket and held it out to Harry.

"Give them to Samson."

Samson took the key.

"Go and find the paperwork. I'm sure Roger won't be stupid while you're away."

"No, no. I'll be good."

Three minutes later, Samson walked in, holding the documents.

Harry produced a gold pen from his inside jacket pocket and gave it to Roger. "Make it out in the name of Hunter Enterprises."

Roger wrote down the details as best he could with his shaking hand.

"There you go." Roger passed over the completed documents and made a point to return the gold pen. He didn't want to get into any more trouble than he already was.

Harry checked the documents carefully, folded them, and, together with the pen, placed them into his inside pocket. "It's a pleasure doing business with you. Now Samson, remind our friend what we do to people who cross us."

A big grin spread across the giant's face as he watched Roger's expression turn to one of horror.

"No, please. Don't do anything where it'll show. I've got an audition for a part in a film next week."

The blind angle of the massive left hook meant Roger never saw it coming as it pounded into the right side of his face. The punch took out three of his teeth and rattled his entire head, taking him down to the floor, unconscious before he landed.

Roger was by no means the first person to experience the power of Samson's left hand. He loved using it because it's probably the most potent punch any boxer can inflict.

The left hook gets its power from a full-body rotation. Instead of being powered by the straight tricep like a right hand, the left hook relies on the shoulder, chest and bicep muscles to swing the hook across your opponent's jaw. In the boxing ring, it's usually the knockout blow.

Samson lifted the badly battered and unconscious man and carried him down the stairs over his shoulder.

Harry used the key fob to open the boot of the vehicle he had just acquired, and Samson dropped the body in.

An hour later, Roger began to stir. His head felt like it had been run over by a train. He opened his eyes and looked around. His vision was hazy. All he could see was a mesh of small metal squares in front of him. He looked down and saw his feet and lower legs were secured by nylon rope to a metal girder. On each side of him a sheet of board, marked with the word 'GypLyner'.

He lifted his aching head to see Harry standing in front of him. Samson at his side.

Harry grinned. "Ah, Roger. Back with us at last. Now let's see if you can act your way out of this."

Roger looked quizzically as the two men applied the final sheet of GypLyner to the front of the column, and his world went dark.

The next sound Roger heard was the bolts being added, effectively sealing him in.

From above, he heard the sound of a loud engine being switched on, then felt something dripping onto his head.

Then, as the noise of the engine increased, it dawned on him what was about to happen.

All he could do was scream his lungs out as the thick sludge of concrete rained down, slowly getting higher and higher. As it reached his head, he scrunched his eyes closed. There was nothing he could do except pray.

On the outside of the column, a smile crept across Harry's face, which turned into an almost uncontrollable belly laugh, so much so that his body bent forward, and he had to put his hand across his stomach. He just about managed to get the words out.

"There you go, Roger!" he shouted. "You wanted a part in a film. I've given you the leading role. Like in the movies. You're going to die hard."

CHAPTER TWO

DAVE REX

Thursday 12th October 2006

Dave Rex ambles away from the food truck. His mouth is literally salivating over the double cheeseburger he's just purchased. As he goes to take the first bite, he catches a glimpse of a man and woman standing at his market stall. Usually, the chance of potential customers would be a welcome sight. However, what he sees on this occasion makes the burger slip from his fingers to embellish the pathway and cover his footwear in ketchup.

It's the words 'Trading Standards' emblazoned across the back of their jackets. Instantly, he changes direction and scuttles away, knowing his speedy departure will allow them to seize his stock and the cash box with his day's takings.

Shit.

Maybe this is the sign that's been niggling away at him for the past few weeks. Telling him it's time to get out of the fake designer clothes business.

Sure, it pays the bills, but he isn't exactly making a

fortune. Besides, it's all going online nowadays. Run by a younger crowd who are savvy about computers and websites and stuff he has no knowledge of or particular interest in.

The loss of his stock and takings is one thing. But to add insult to injury, today is his fortieth birthday.

This was not the kind of surprise he'd been hoping for.

Dave's intention had been to use the day's takings and treat himself to a delicious meal at a fancy restaurant. The arrival of the two uninvited guests means his budget won't stretch to the sizzle of a nice juicy steak. Instead, he's reduced to chomping on the contents of a supermarket economy tin of baked beans.

As he sits on the grimy mattress in his tiny bedsit, a shiver of revulsion courses through him. He reaches over and picks up a bottle of his favourite tipple, Jack Daniel's, hoping to lift the gloom. When he pours out the contents, there's barely enough to coat the bottom of his glass. It's the final insult.

He lights the spliff he rolled earlier. As it takes effect, he has an idea. His old pal Bernie is the laziest person he's ever met, but he always seems to have a bundle of cash in his pocket. All from a bit of dealing.

Dave recalls the phrase Bernie has bored him with a thousand times. Finally, it seems to have penetrated his mind.

"You're missing out, Dave," he's forever saying. "People always enjoy a bit of weed."

CHAPTER THREE

JAMES SHELDON

October 2008

There are four of us standing in the basement car park of Trentbridge police station. It's an early start. Seven o'clock. We're about to carry out a raid on a suspected drug dealer's house.

The man in charge of the operation is Detective Inspector Phil Jones.

"Right. Listen up. The person we're after is Johnny Dixon. The file shows he was released two weeks ago. We've had reliable information he has been seen dealing at various nightclubs and bars. As far as we're aware, the target lives alone."

The DI hands round a photo of the suspect for us all to see, then turns to me. "DS Sheldon, I want you to cover the side door." He turns to the young female officer. "PC Turner, you cover the back garden. PC Zander and I will go in the front. It's a two-up, two-down end-of-terrace. Should be a routine bust. Any questions?"

PC Zander raises his hand. "What if we find someone else at the property?"

"If we find drugs, we arrest them as well."

Half an hour later, we're in position. I hear three loud thumps as PC Zander uses his enforcer to batter down the front door.

Seconds later, I hear PC Turner call out, "He's climbing out the upstairs window."

I run round to the back just in time to see a figure jump down onto the grass, landing four feet from PC Turner.

I recognise the man from the photo. It's Johnny Dixon. I notice something glint from his wrist. Then I watch helplessly as he produces a gun.

"Watch out, Elaine!" I shout, but as she approaches the man, he shoots her in the chest, knocking her backwards several feet.

Dixon runs down the garden while I rush to help Elaine. I'm cradling her in my arms as Zander and Jones come running from the house.

I watch PC Zander bravely run after the gunman, but before he can get near him, Dixon disappears over the wall at the far end of the garden.

Not wanting to take my hands away from the gushing wound, I shout out to DI Jones, "Call an ambulance!"

I'm desperately applying pressure to the wound to stop the bleeding, but there's so much of it. I try my best to reassure her. "It's okay, Elaine. Help's on the way. Everything's going to be all right. You'll be fine."

I hear the siren of the ambulance but feel her body give a

shudder, then she goes limp, her eyes close, and her head falls to the side.

I cry out. “Stay with me, Elaine,” But it’s obvious there’s nothing anyone can do to save her.

I gently lay her head on the grass, remove my suit jacket, and place it over her.

I sit on the grass, covered in the blood of a brave female police officer who, at just nineteen, has given her life in the pursuit of justice.

CHAPTER FOUR

JAMES

By the time we get back to the station, word had spread about our fallen colleague. Every phone is ringing; calls from police officers on their day off or on a later shift volunteering to come to work and help locate Johnny Dixon. No stone will be left unturned to find the person responsible for the death of one of their own.

The incident room is packed. There are more people than I've seen here before. Everyone looks up as Larry Archer enters the room and walks over to the incident board.

"Okay. Listen up, everyone. First of all, I want to thank all of you who have given up your free time to come in. The media have just put out a broadcast for Johnny Dixon with his photo. We can expect the phones to start ringing any minute now. So, I'm opening six more phone lines to cope with the expected increase. We can only hope someone calls in with some solid information."

The DCI turns to me. "James, I want you to take two firearms officers and check at Dixon's mum's and his sister's places. Then pay a visit to his old girlfriend. It's probably a longshot. I can't see that she'd wait around two years for that toerag, but you never know. See if his family or the girlfriend know anything. Maybe one of them can give us the names of some of his old associates."

Twenty minutes later, I'm in an unmarked police vehicle heading off to Jervison Street.

We park a few yards from number eight and walk up the pathway. The two officers with me are carrying their weapons out of sight in side holsters underneath their jackets.

I knock at the door. The woman who answers the door looks to be in her late forties. She shows no surprise when I hold up my ID badge.

"Hello, Mrs Dixon. I'm DS James Sheldon."

"If you're expecting to find him here, I can tell you now, you're wasting your time. This is the last place he'd come. I've had nothing to do with him since he was released."

"In that case, Mrs Dixon, would you mind if we come in and have a look around?"

The woman steps back. "I have nothing to hide."

"Is there anyone else in the house, Mrs Dixon?"

"No. I live alone."

I turn to the two officers. "Okay, boys."

They go inside. I gently put my hand on the lady's sleeve. "I think it best if we stand outside for a minute."

The officers cautiously make their way along the hall,

checking each room. Once they are satisfied, they slowly go up the stairs, guns poised.

"They won't find anything."

"I believe you, but we have to be sure."

Mrs Dixon turns to me. "I'm so sorry for the family of that poor girl. To think my son was responsible makes me sick. Growing up, he was such a sweet boy. Then he got into drugs, and I didn't recognise him after that."

"You can't be held responsible for his actions."

The two officers walk down the stairs, weapons returned to their holsters.

"Looks like you were right, Mrs Dixon. We'll get out of your way. And remember what I said. It's the drugs that are responsible. I'm sure you're a great mum. Take care of yourself."

CHAPTER FIVE

JAMES

The next address on our list is Percy Street. It turns out to be a modest terraced house. Compared to the others, it looks in need of some TLC. The paintwork is peeling, and the grass is overgrown.

As we did at the last address, I walk a couple of paces in front of the armed officers. I press the bell but don't hear it ring inside the house, so I knock, to be greeted with a barking dog. By the sound of it, a large dog.

One of the armed officers pipes up. "Oh shit. I hate dogs."

I look at him. He's six feet tall and well-built. "You hate dogs?"

"Well, no. I don't hate them. What I mean is I'm just not comfortable around them."

Luckily, the conversation is interrupted when the door opens. Dixon's sister, who looks to be in her early thirties, stands there.

I hold up my ID badge. "Hello. I'm DS James Sheldon. These officers are—"

The woman lets out a gasp.

I turn to follow where her eyes are looking.

One of the armed officers has the butt of his gun in sight under his jacket.

"Put that away," I tell him in no uncertain terms.

"I'm sorry," I tell the lady.

She seems to recover a little. "My mum just phoned me, so I know why you've come. He's not here."

"I understand but we really do need to find your brother. Is it okay if we come in and take a look around?"

"Mum said the best way was to cooperate with you. I've nothing to hide. But be careful in the kitchen; I've just taken the washing out of the machine. I don't need you making a mess. Understand."

"Yes. We'll be careful. I promise. Now, is there anyone else in the house?"

"No. My husband's at work. It's just me."

"We heard a dog?"

"He's in the backyard."

"Is there a shed there?"

"What? No. The garden's tiny. Just a kennel. Why? Do you think my brother's hiding in the dog's kennel?"

Her comment and the way she says it makes me laugh. "No. It's just we need to be certain."

"You're welcome to search it if you want. I'm sure Nelson will have an objection. But it's your call."

"That won't be necessary."

"Okay. Now, if you wouldn't mind waiting outside with me while the two officers undertake a search. I'm sure they'll be careful with your clean washing."

The armed officers take two steps into the hallway, taking their time over each step.

I stand with the lady outside the front door, making sure her back is to the house. This way she can't see as the two officers unclip their weapons.

After a couple of minutes they appear back in the hall.

The armed officers take each step slowly as they climb the stairs.

After searching upstairs, they make their way back down, ensuring their weapons are out of sight.

"Nothing here," one of them states.

I turn to the lady. "Thank you, Mrs Jamison. We appreciate your cooperation. Here's my card. If your brother gets in touch, or you have any information that will help us find him, I'd appreciate a call."

The lady takes the card and glances at the details. "I can't believe my brother would do such a thing. He's been hanging out with a rough crowd but..."

"I know it's hard to comprehend, but we do believe he's the person responsible."

"Growing up, we were close, you know. Always playing together in the park. For my brother to shoot someone, let alone a police officer. I won't accept it until he tells me himself."

I don't tell her I was there and witnessed her brother shoot Elaine. It wouldn't do any good, and Mrs Jamison seems like a decent woman, so there's no need to upset her further.

As we walk to our vehicle, one of the officers taps his jacket pockets.

"Lost something?"

"Yeah. I thought I had a couple of shortbread biscuits left."

I look at him, trying to keep a straight face.

"You sure you didn't leave them as a treat for the dog?"

CHAPTER SIX

JAMES

Two down, one to go. The girlfriend. Vicky Chance lives in the top-floor flat at 23 Cavendish Street.

I'm about to get out of the car when my phone buzzes. It's DCI Larry Archer.

"Hi, James. We checked the visitor records and Vicky visited him for about a year. Then nothing. I guess we can assume she got fed up and moved on to someone else. Can't say I blame her. Anyway. It's worth a try. She might be able to suggest somewhere he could have gone. But go in as if he might be there."

"Okay, Guv. Will do."

I go up to the front door of the house. The sign by the bell reads 'Top Floor Flat – Chance'.

I try the front door. It's unlocked. I make my way up to the top, closely tailed by the armed officers.

Once at the door of the flat, I knock three times. No answer. I wait a few seconds, then knock again. This time a little harder.

After a short while, I hear a female voice. "Hello. Who is it?"

"This is the police. Can you open the door please?"

The armed officers and I move to the side. There's always the chance of someone shooting through the door, and police training teaches you this. Just in case.

I hear the chain being slid across, then the door opens a few inches. I hold up my ID badge so it can be seen.

After glancing at it for a few seconds, the female opens the door fully. "You can't be too careful nowadays."

"Vicky Chance?"

"Yes, that's me."

"Vicky. Not to alarm you, but I have two armed police officers with me. You're aware of the recent shooting of a female police officer?"

"Yes. I heard it on the news."

"We have reason to believe your boyfriend, Johnny Dixon, is responsible. And we think he's still armed. Hence our caution."

"He's not my boyfriend anymore. I haven't seen him for about a year."

"Would it be possible to come in and have a look around?"

"I'm telling you he's not here."

"I perfectly understand, but we have to check for ourselves. It will literally take a couple of minutes."

"Don't you believe me?"

"I'm sure you're telling us the truth. But what if he's here and has threatened you into saying you haven't seen him? We really do need to see for ourselves. As I say, it will literally take a couple of minutes, then we'll be gone. Otherwise we'll have to go and get a search warrant and come back. This way, we both save time."

The woman seems to think for a moment.

I interject. "It did take you a little while to answer the door. He could have been threatening you."

"I was in the bathroom. I just finished washing my hair. Look. Okay. Come in."

"What I need you to do is come and stand in the hallway with me. It gives the two officers a clear path so they can look around without the chance of you getting hurt."

Vicky steps into the hallway.

The armed officers make their way in.

"I'm sorry about this, but we have to check everyone associated with Johnny."

"As I said, we split up. I haven't seen him for about a year."

The two officers return. "All clear. No sign he's been here."

The last sentence is code. Unlike his sister, who said she lived with her husband, the suspect's mother and girlfriend told us they live alone. It means the officers will have checked in the bathroom to see if there are things like a man's razor or shaving foam. In the bedroom they will have checked for men's clothing.

But I'm not convinced. Something she said doesn't sound right.

"Would it be okay if I use your bathroom quickly?" I ask. "Too many coffees."

She nods. "Through the lounge, down the hallway, the door on the right."

I rush over, trying to make it look like I need to go. I close the bathroom door, lift up the toilet seat, then look around. I look at the bath. It has a shower attachment. The bottom of the bath is wet.

Then, I notice something glinting on the shelf with the shampoo and conditioner. I recognise it because my wife bought me a similar one for Christmas a couple of years ago. It's a BOSS men's steel metal link bracelet.

I don't use the toilet but flush it and wash my hands, then walk back into the lounge. "Okay, Vicky. Thank you for allowing us to have a look around. It's obvious he's not here. So we'll be on our way. One last thing. You stopped going to visit Johnny a year ago. Do you have a new boyfriend?"

"No. I just didn't want anything to do with him. I'm happier on my own."

We make our way downstairs and over to the car. I start the engine and drive off.

Once we're a couple of streets away, I pull over.

"Did you notice something we missed?" asks one of the officers.

"There was a man's bracelet on a shelf with the toiletries above the bath. She said she doesn't have a boyfriend. She also said she took her time answering the door because she was washing her hair. But it was dry and didn't look like it had been brushed today. Even if her hair had dried, she would still have brushed it. And on the landing, I noticed a hatch on the ceiling. I think it leads to a loft, and he's hiding up there."

I take out my phone, call DCI Archer, and tell him what I suspect.

"Well spotted, James. I'll contact the prison and get a list of the items he was booked out with on his release. Hopefully, it includes a silver bracelet."

I return to the station. As I'm about to sit at my desk, my boss calls me over.

"I've just heard back from the prison. The property release form Dixon signed included a silver bracelet. I've spoken to the ACC, and he's arranging a search warrant for us to go in tomorrow morning."

The heavy boot of a police officer kicks down the front door and two armed officers enter the flat of Vicky Chance. One calls out. "ARMED POLICE. STAY WHERE YOU ARE."

Both officers make their way to the bedroom. The girlfriend is laid out on the bed. Johnny is kneeling next to her; he reaches across to his trousers on a nearby chair. As he raises his arm, gun in hand, one of the officers yells out, "STOP OR I'LL SHOOT."

Maybe it's the drugs, maybe the adrenaline of the moment, whatever the reason, Johnny continues to raise his weapon.

As two bullets enter his head, his girlfriend screams.

The officers move forward. One of them drags the girl into the hallway while the other keeps his weapon trained on the lifeless body of the man they came to arrest. The officer's training has taught him that you don't take any chances. He will remain, gun trained, until a medic can pronounce life extinct.

The officer kicks Johnny's gun across the room. It's picked up by another officer who places it into an evidence bag.

It's not the result we would have preferred, but Johnny's actions left the officer with no choice.

The two firearms officers will be subject to the internal investigation that always happens when someone is killed during an operation.

CHAPTER SEVEN

DAVE

Over the past two years, Dave Rex has seen his lifestyle transformed. Proof of Bernie's words of wisdom. People certainly do enjoy a bit of weed. It's why every week Dave visits his friend to buy more. Thanks to Bernie, the days of scraping a living trying to shift dodgy designer gear are long gone.

Drug dealing has enabled Dave to move out of his seedy little bedsit into a luxury apartment in a more upmarket area of town. And it's allowed his taste for the finer things to surface: nice restaurants, golfing holidays to Spain, and appointments with a local tailor.

Perhaps the Trading Standards raid on his market stall wasn't such a bad thing after all.

One evening, as Dave drives away from Bernie's house, a car pulls out sharply and blocks his way. Dave snarls, "What the fuck are you doing, you stupid bastard?"

Another car draws up close behind him with its headlights on full beam, blinding him. Someone gets out and walks towards him. Dave winds down the window.

"What the bloody hell is going—?"

The man holds up an ID badge.

"Police. You're under arrest on suspicion of the possession of Class A drugs with the intent to supply."

Dave's heart sinks: just when he thought his luck had changed.

It's the day before Dave's court appearance. He's been charged with possession of cannabis with intent to supply, a criminal offence under the Misuse of Drugs Act 1971.

Dave sits, glumly looking across the beautifully polished mahogany desk, taking pride of place in his barrister's office. The man looks suitably dapper in his dark blue suit with its subtle thin pinstripe. It's what you can afford when you charge seven hundred pounds an hour.

He leans back in his leather office chair, with his elbows on the armrests, holding a pen at each end between his finger and thumb as he speaks.

"Now, Mr Rex, from what you've told me, in your younger days, you were questioned regarding several offences. These include burglary, robbery, assault, arson, and receiving stolen goods."

A smile appears across Dave's face. Because he knows, in truth, it's a much longer rap sheet.

The barrister continues. "However, as none of these alleged offences have ever led to a conviction, the prosecution won't be able to refer to them. You go before the court with a clean record. That will certainly help our case.

"Furthermore, the CPS has agreed to take into account the fact you're prepared to testify against your supplier, Bernard Yates. The police will ask the judge to take that into account in sentencing. It won't be announced in open court, so no one else will hear about it."

Dave can only hope this highly paid la-de-dah barrister is skilful enough to persuade the judge to go easy.

Maybe, if he's lucky, his sentence will only be a year, and with good behaviour, he'll be out in six months.

Dave stands in the dock, dressed in a smart plain blue suit and tie, as the barrister advised. He looks across the court at the stern-faced judge, decked out in the resplendent regalia of his formal robes.

"Mr Rex. This court has found you guilty of intent to supply a controlled drug. A serious charge, and, as such, it is my duty to pass sentence."

Dave mentally prepares himself for his fate. He knows what's coming. He's about to lose the comforts of the luxury apartment that he's come to enjoy.

The judge continues. "I hereby sentence you to four years in prison."

It looks like, for the foreseeable future, Dave will be spending up to twenty-three hours a day in a ten-by-ten cell. And with the current prison overcrowding situation, he probably won't be alone. He'll be forced to share the tiny space with a sweaty companion. Swapping the comfort of his luxurious king-size memory foam mattress for the cramped space upper level of a metal bunk bed.

And to top it all, after two years of *Haute cuisine*, he must now resign himself to the questionable delights of prison grub.

Dave's thoughts return to the courtroom as the judge pauses and looks down to consult his notes. "However... I have heard the mitigating evidence put forward by your barrister."

Dave crosses his fingers and holds his breath as the judge looks directly at him.

"Mr Rex. I can see how you might have been sucked into this by someone you considered to be a friend. I take into account the fact that you have no previous convictions. It is obvious you find yourself in the court today as a result of mixing in the company of a bad crowd..."

Dave listens intently to the final words of High Court Judge Andrew Benton-Wright.

"...I trust the opportunity that I am bestowing on you today will allow you to mend your ways. I hope there will be no need to see you in this court again."

Dave walks out with his sentence suspended for two years. But by the time he reaches the street, the judge's summing-up speech is a distant memory.

After such a close encounter, Dave vows one thing to himself. It will be the last time the police will be able to pin anything on him. He's hired someone he's known for years: Kenny Green, who used to help him out from time to time when he was running the fake designer clothes business.

Dave has made him his second-in-command. In truth, he's really just the patsy. If someone's going to get caught with the drugs, it certainly won't be Dave. He has plans. Big plans.

CHAPTER EIGHT

DAVE

It's been twelve months since his court appearance and Dave hasn't wasted any time in making good on his plans.

Thanks to Dave testifying against him in court, Bernie is currently banged up for the next twelve years. This means Dave has been able to take over his old pal's drug business – Lock, Stock, and Weed!

So, gone are the days of selling to the junkies. He's moved up the pecking order to supplying local wholesalers.

He's found a new supplier. Mohammad Awan is a large-scale cannabis dealer from London who doesn't like to do business on his 'home patch'.

He prefers to deal with people in the Midlands area. This is handy because his brother lives in Birmingham.

For their monthly meetings, Dave spends an hour travelling down the M6 motorway, with Kenny Green following close behind in his own car.

Meanwhile, Mohammad heads up from London. They meet at his brother's restaurant. It's in an area referred to as the Balti Triangle, just south of Birmingham's city centre.

After the three men have finished their meal, Kenny leaves and drives back to Trentbridge with the 'merchandise' hidden in the boot of his car.

Once Kenny's safely on his way, Dave and Mohammad walk through to the private office at the back of the restaurant. They sit and conclude their affairs over a cup of tea.

Today, Dave has questions he's wanted to ask for a couple of months.

"Mohammad, I wonder if you can offer me some advice. What's the best way to hide all the cash and make it look like it's come from a legal source?"

"Yes, of course, my friend. I'll be most happy to help. To avoid attracting attention, you need to look and act like a businessman. Use legitimate businesses as a cover for your more lucrative enterprise. This will enable you to enjoy a good lifestyle without arousing suspicion from the police or the tax man.

"Take me, for example; I own four mini convenience stores, a betting shop, and a car wash. Each had been a business on the edge of going bankrupt. I have used the cash from my under-the-counter enterprise and bought them one by one. So, if anyone looks into my affairs, it will look like I bought each one for a small amount. Then turned them into a highly profitable business.

"Of course, it means I must pay tax. But my accountant is astute, so it works out at about fifteen per cent, which I consider a good investment.

"I suggest you start by looking for a business that's not making any money. Buy it cheap and make it look like you've turned it into a profitable business. Then, use the profits to invest in another one and do the same.

"My advice is to build several different types of businesses as fast as possible. Grow them to the level where it looks like they support your lifestyle. The most important thing is to ensure they are the type of business that takes most of their money in cash."

Dave listens intently, and the more he hears, the more he realises it makes complete sense.

He recalls a friend recently telling him about a takeaway kebab shop that was on the market. He mentioned the owner was hoping for a quick cash sale. At the time, Dave hadn't taken much notice, but now he could see it might be the perfect answer to his problem.

On his return to Trentbridge, Dave contacts the owner and arranges to view the takeaway.

"I called you earlier about the business."

"What can I tell you?" the owner says. "I've been here for eight years. It's a good business with reliable staff. It virtually runs itself."

"How much profit does it make?"

"Well, if you look at the accounts, they show it makes a loss. But, between you and me, that's because I take money out in cash to avoid the tax."

"So how much do you want for this business that doesn't make any money?"

"For a quick sale, I'd take fifteen thousand."

"You must be joking. I'll give you five cash."

"No, no. Make it ten, and we've got a deal. I need a quick sale."

"I've changed my mind. Not interested."

The man looks depressed as Dave starts to walk away. "Okay, okay. I'll take your offer of five."

"I offered you five, and you turned it down. But now you're prepared to take it. That tells me you're desperate. My offer is now four thousand cash. Say yes, or I'm going to walk away. There are plenty more opportunities around."

The man looks like he's about to cry. "Okay, okay. I'll take it. How soon can we do the deal?"

Dave pulls out his phone and calls his lawyer. "Mark Jackson please. It's Dave Rex... Hello, Mark. I'm buying a takeaway business. How soon can you draw up an agreement...? Yeah, that would be perfect. I'll call your secretary later with the details."

Dave turns to the seller, who is looking at him anxiously. "My lawyer says he can have the paperwork ready by lunchtime tomorrow. The cash is no problem. We can meet at three and finalise everything."

The following afternoon, Dave becomes the proud new owner of Hanley Kebabs, situated at 301 Woolston Road.

It doesn't matter if the place is losing money. It will make the perfect front for his illegal activities.

It means Dave has taken his first step to becoming an *honest* entrepreneur.

CHAPTER NINE

DAVE

Dave Rex is a very happy bunny. Ever since he bought the takeaway kebab shop, things have been going exceptionally well for him.

He's reorganised the staff, so the business makes money on its own. And it makes even more after he pumps in the cash from his drugs empire.

In fact, things are going so well that last week, he bought his second business, a company called Trent Taxis. He's also purchased a luxury apartment in the Brampton Manor gated complex. It's only a couple of streets away from Hanford Court Retirement Village, where his dear old mum lives. He's paying a small fortune for the place, but she's worth it. She's the only family he's got.

And he's made the decision to expand into selling Class A drugs. This is in response to constant requests from the people he supplies with cannabis.

He asked Mohammad, who was more than happy to put him in touch with a supplier who, he assures Dave, can be trusted implicitly.

That's why, this morning, Dave has driven a hundred and seventy miles down the motorway.

Right now, he's standing open-mouthed in front of an absolutely breathtaking period property. It's so impressive that at first, he thought he was staring at the Bank of England building. The setting seems so unreal to be discussing drug deals – then it dawns on him: serviced offices in London come in many forms.

He double-checks the address. Yes, it's the right place: 1 Royal Exchange, City of London. This has to be one of the grandest and most iconic buildings in the whole of London.

Dave slowly climbs the nine steps, eclipsed by a portico of eight Corinthian columns, each standing forty feet tall. He can't help but gaze up at them as he approaches the plush entrance.

Once inside, he makes his way across the dark oak herringbone parquet floor. With each step, he can hear the soft echo of his footwear bouncing off the walls as he saunters towards the reception desk. It's so tall he can only make out the head and shoulders of the young woman sitting behind it.

"Good morning, sir. How may I help you?"

"My name is Dave Rex. I have a ten o'clock appointment with Mr Fedorov of Kazan Imports."

"Certainly, sir. I'll let him know you're here. If you'd like to take a seat..." She points towards a plush orange-coloured leather sofa.

Dave sits and glances at the round clock on the opposite wall: precisely five minutes to ten.

He recalls what Mohammad told him at their last meeting: "These guys are Russians. The product they supply is first class, and they will never let you down. For them, it is all about business. I know you are reliable and professional. But be warned, these are not people you ever want to get on the wrong side of."

Dave thanked Mohammad but almost instantly dismissed his words. He is used to dealing with dodgy people. *Russians, so what? No big deal, nothing I can't handle!*

Now he is at this swanky address, and even before he has met these people, he can sense they are in a different league.

He feels the palms of his hands. It usually takes a lot to make him sweat.

"Mr Rex, if you would care to follow me..."

Dave notices the young receptionist standing in front of him.

She leads him across to the central lifts and presses the button. The twin glass doors open with a quiet swish.

"It's the third floor. Mr Fedorov will meet you there."

A few seconds after departing the ground floor, there is a ding, and the doors open. Two large muscular men are standing by the lift, one on each side. They look like a pair of gorillas and seem out of place in their smart black suits.

Dave tries to calm himself with a rare thought of humour: *I bet they had three shredded wheat for breakfast.*

One of them speaks. "Follow please."

He leads the way while the other walks behind Dave. The idea is obviously to make him feel uncomfortable. *It's working.*

Dave is led into a small office. Once inside, the door closes.

"We will search you."

There is no question of allowing Dave to object.

One gorilla stands facing Dave. The other pats him

down, starting at the shoulders and going all the way to his ankles. Front, sides and back – extremely professional.

As Dave studies the men, he thinks they must be ex-forces, Russian military.

Satisfied Dave is *clean*, the gorilla facing him speaks.

"Mr Fedorov will see you now." They lead Dave to another room. The sign outside announces 'Meeting Room'.

One of the goons opens the door and signals for Dave to enter. He walks in and approaches the figure standing by the large round dark walnut table. Behind him, he hears the click of the door being locked.

"Ah, Mr Rex. Welcome."

The man holds out his hand, a broad smile across his face. Dave had expected to make a good impression by wearing his very best suit. Sadly, upon meeting Mr Fedorov, he's dismayed to discover it's no match for the pure craftsmanship and delicate cut of Savile Row tailoring.

"It is good to meet you. Our mutual friend, Mohammad, speaks very highly of you."

"Thank you, Mr Fedorov. That's nice to know."

"Please, you call me Vladimir." A hint of Moscow is still detectable through the English accent. "You've had a long journey this morning. Can I get you something to drink?"

"That's very kind, but I had a coffee just before I got here." Dave tries to keep his voice steady and confident.

Vladimir sits at the table and beckons for Dave to do the same.

The two men get down to business. Vladimir asks him several questions, some of them awkward. Dave feels compelled to answer them honestly. He reveals things he wouldn't normally tell anyone.

At the end of the questioning, Vladimir looks pleased.

"I understand you are from Trentbridge?"

"Yeah. Lived there all my life."

"Yes. I've been there a few times. We used to deal with someone who was based there. A very astute gentleman. I think he decided to move into the property business. Therefore, David, I think we can do business. Here is the deal."

Mohammad was right. Dave can see these people are serious players. It is forcibly brought home to him that he must always arrive on time at the agreed handovers and be professional in every way.

Dave agrees to take a shipment every two weeks. Each consignment will be for ten thousand pounds.

Dave's empire is growing rapidly. And woe betide anyone who tries to stand in his way.

CHAPTER TEN

THE FAB FOUR

Wednesday 24th November 2010

Chief Inspector Larry Archer is sitting in his office. He stretches across his desk and places the last of seven reports into the out-tray. He glances at his watch – it's just after two-thirty, and all his paperwork for the day is complete. He sighs with relief.

As a reward, he's about to go and make a coffee, maybe treat himself to a couple of digestive biscuits. He stands but is interrupted by his phone ringing.

"Hello, DCI Archer."

The voice that follows is little more than a whisper. "Okay. As long as you can offer me the deal you promised, I'll give you all the details you need. Names, bank accounts, the bloody lot. But I can't be seen coming into the police station."

"Where do you propose we meet?"

"You know the old abandoned car workshop on Clare Road?"

"Yes, I know it."

"Meet me there in an hour. There's a gate at the side. I'll leave it unlocked."

"See you there."

Larry walks over to the kitchen area, pours some water into the kettle and grabs his jar of coffee, only to find it's empty. He picks up the biscuit barrel clearly marked 'Larry's biscuits'. They've been nabbed as well.

He strolls back to his office and glances out of the window. The weather isn't looking great, typical for late November. He grabs his coat and gloves and walks towards the lift.

If he leaves now, he'll have time to grab a coffee at the Red Brick Café, pop into the newsagents, and pick up a newspaper and a packet of digestives.

The route from his office takes him past the desk of a junior female colleague.

"Going out in this weather, sir?"

"Yes, I know." He shivers dramatically. "But it could be a big break. I'm off to meet a whistle-blower about the council corruption case."

"Congratulations, sir. If anyone needs to contact you, what do I tell them?"

"Don't tell them anything. It's hush-hush. I'm meeting this person at the old vehicle workshop on Clare Road. He's promised to give me inside information on the dodgy developer. We'll finally have the bastard. If anyone needs me, tell them I'll be back in a couple of hours. But first, I'm off to grab a coffee and some bickies. Someone's emptied my biscuit tin. You'd think they'd be safe in a bloody police station, wouldn't you!"

The female officer laughs.

Larry walks over to the lift, presses the button and hears the creaking sound of the rusty unoiled cables. As he stands waiting, DCI Gerry Payne passes by and stops for a quick exchange.

"Hi, Gerry. How's it going?"

"Not bad. I think we're getting somewhere with that stabbing on Federation Road. How about you?"

"Might have a break re. the council fraud. Off to meet with someone. It could crack the case wide open."

The lift arrives with a ding.

"Good luck."

"Thanks, Gerry."

The following day

Assistant Chief Constable Adrian Pratt walks into the CID office. He finds Phil Jones sitting at his desk. "Ah, DI Jones."

"Yes, sir?"

"Have you seen DCI Archer?"

"Not since yesterday, sir."

"When you do, ask him to come to my office."

"Of course, sir."

It's been a long day for Detective Inspector Phil Jones. He's been at work since seven. He glances at the office clock and sees it's just after six. Another hour and he'll call it a day.

His phone extension rings, and he lifts it to his ear, but before he can utter a word, a bad-tempered voice blasts down the line.

"I thought I told you to get DCI Archer to come to my office."

"He's not been in all day, sir. We've been trying to contact him, but he left his mobile in his office. No one's seen him since yesterday."

"That's unacceptable. Find him. NOW!"

Phil is left listening to the dial tone, his ear still ringing.

Hmmm, he thinks. *Pratt by name, Pratt by nature!*

CHAPTER ELEVEN

JAMES

February 2012

It's been fifteen months since the disappearance of DCI Larry Archer. I miss having him around. He was my mentor. He taught me so much.

DCI Gerry Payne, DI Phil Jones, and I initially investigated his disappearance when he failed to turn up for work after two days.

At first, we thought he might be ill. That was until Tracy, his sixteen-year-old daughter, came looking for him. Then, we knew something was wrong.

We spent weeks reviewing all his case files, trying to find someone who might have held a grudge and wanted revenge. It was a long list.

Then we went over the cases he was working on when he disappeared. He had mentioned to Gerry that he was going to meet an informant. So our main line of inquiry was to find who he'd met. The only problem was that the last call to his mobile had been from a phone box on Clare Road.

It wasn't easy because we were all up to our eyes dealing with other cases. There was a drug epidemic caused by a new product called Monkey Dust that was selling for less than five pounds a hit and was more potent than heroin.

We were watching all the local drug dealers to see who was supplying it, but everyone seemed to be tight-lipped.

On top of that, we had a situation where, six months after DCI Larry Archer disappeared, all the files related to cases he was working on went missing.

For some time, rumours had circulated that one or two of the local drug dealers had an informant on the inside. Someone passing information about forthcoming drug raids and details of surveillance operations. The main suspects were a couple of police officers close to retirement, who were probably trying to enhance their pension.

The drug squad had undertaken three raids on different premises. We had expected to find large quantities of drugs. However, on each occasion, the amount found was so small that the only charge we could make was for personal possession. It was obvious they knew in advance that we were coming.

We also had the news that DI Phil Jones had decided to take early retirement to start his own private investigation agency. I guess I didn't blame him. The past year had seemed like a downward spiral. This time last year, we celebrated being at the top of our game.

The night before DCI Archer disappeared, we had been attending the Police Federation Awards Ceremony.

I replay the moment in my head.

The Commissioner of the Metropolitan Police stepped up to the podium.

"Ladies and Gentleman, it gives me great pleasure to

announce the award for the Detective Investigation of the Year. This year, it goes to... Trentbridge."

DCI Larry Archer, DCI Gerry Payne, DI Phil Jones, and I stood and made our way to the front and onto the stage to collect the award.

It was given for our investigation into a nasty gang of criminals who trafficked people from their home country of Latvia. Luring them here with false promises of a better life.

Following the long and painstaking investigation, the five people behind the operation were brought before the courts. They each received sentences of between three and six years. Even the judge commented on our presented evidence, calling it 'outstanding'.

The winner's plaque was held high in the air as the four of us returned to our table.

We had been known as the Fab Four because our clear-up rates were far above the national average. Yet here we were, just a year later, with Larry gone and Phil Jones on the brink of leaving.

It makes me wonder what the next twelve months will bring.

CHAPTER TWELVE

DAVE

February 2012

As Dave arrives at the Fenton Motel café for his fortnightly drugs handover, the hairs on the back of his neck begin to stand on end. It's the sight of the Russian boss sitting in place of one of the usual goons.

Vladimir is quick to hold out his hand and offer a smile as if to reassure him. He speaks in his smooth but not-quite-perfect English.

"David. It is lovely to see you again. We have been doing business for long time, yes?"

Dave smiles and nods.

"The reason for my visit is to offer you a new proposition. We have lovely girls we can offer you for five hundred pounds a week. If you don't have experience setting up an escort agency, we will send people to help. You can double or even triple your money. Ten girls can make you five thousand a week. And perks? You get free companionship. You want to think it over and let my people know next time?"

Dave is relieved this is the reason behind the Russian boss's unexpected appearance. "It sounds like a very interesting proposition, Vladimir. I will certainly give it serious thought."

The two men continue chatting, but there's something on Dave's mind. Finally, he plucks up the courage.

"Vladimir. I'm curious. I've often wondered how you knew about this motel. It seems the perfect place to conduct our meetings."

"Ah, yes. The man I mentioned in London. He suggested it. Much like yourself, a very astute gentleman."

Vladimir glances at his Rolex. "I must go now but you tell my men the answer at the next meeting. Yes?"

Dave tells Vladimir he will think about it, but, in his mind, he's pretty sure his answer will be yes. He's heard how much money can be made from these Eastern European girls. And the freebies would also be good. They'll probably be used to the kinds of things that turn him on.

Two weeks later, when the next deal goes down, Dave passes on the message that he would like to go ahead with Vladimir's new proposal. The two Russians smile.

"I think you make good decision. I tell boss when we get back to London," one of them says.

March 2012

Within six weeks, Dave has his own escort agency up and running. He starts with ten girls, just as Vladimir suggested. The deal is that the first month is free. After that, he must pay five hundred pounds per week per girl. The Russians add details of the girls to a string of escort and private massage websites. Within hours, the phones are ringing.

Dave finds two cheap rental houses and puts five girls into each, where they sleep. Their work will be undertaken in hotels or at their clients' addresses. They are taken around by drivers from Dave's taxi company.

It doesn't take long for word to spread and demand to increase. Many punters become regular clients.

Dave puts his best girls into their own apartments so they can offer in-calls as well as visits. The cost of the rent will be deducted from their share of the take.

He learns to watch out for girls who lie about their number of clients and try to keep the fees for themselves.

Dave enjoys inflicting pain. Any girl who thinks they can cheat him out of his share soon learns the hard way. One girl who tried bears the scars for life. Since then, word has spread. Now, they are all too terrified to risk it.

CHAPTER THIRTEEN

JAMES

Tuesday 20th March 2012

I crash through the swing doors of the hospital ward with the force of an express train. I stop at the nurses' desk.

I gasp, "Can you tell me which room my wife's in please?"

"Mr Sheldon?"

"Yes, that's right."

"Room three. At the end of the corridor."

"Thank you!" I shout over my shoulder, already ten yards down the corridor. I'm moving at a speed that would make Usain Bolt jealous.

As I reach the doorway, I hear a scream and rush in.

The nurse looks at me.

My wife raises her head. "Where the fuck have you been?"

"So sorry, darling. They only relayed the message to me a few minutes ago."

The midwife looks at Miriam. “He’s here now. No need to hold back any longer.”

Five minutes later, I’m rocking my newborn daughter while the midwife and nurse attend to my wife.

Miriam and I have already decided on a name.

“Hello, Abigail. Welcome to the world. Don’t worry. Daddy’s here to look after you. I promise I’ll always be around to make sure you and your brother Jack are safe.”

I sit next to my wife and lay our baby on the bed between us.

“Give me your phone, and I’ll take a photo,” says one of the nurses.

The camera clicks, and she holds the phone close for us to see.

It’s a beautiful photo of Abigail and two loving parents with beaming smiles.

For now, my job as a detective dealing with criminals and scumbags seems like a different world.

CHAPTER FOURTEEN

HARRY RICHARDSON

Dave Rex was unaware the man Vladimir had referred to as a very astute gentleman was Harry Richardson. Harry had grown up on the Pickstone council estate. He left school with no qualifications and found a job as an apprentice bricklayer.

Shortly after his twentieth birthday, he was involved in a building site accident. Scaffolding collapsed on top of him, and he received seven thousand pounds in compensation.

Rather than buy a car, as his father suggested, he invested the money in a run-down property. He used his skills to make improvements. When he sold it, he almost doubled his money, and that got him hooked on property development.

That was the beginning of what was to become his property empire. At first, it wasn't easy, and even after slogging away for ten years, Harry only owned four properties.

When the economy took a downturn. Harry watched other developers who had overreached themselves financially. Some lost everything. He decided looking at other ways to make money might be a good idea. He sold one of his properties and used the cash to enter the illegal, but very lucrative, drugs market. Over the next seven years, he built a network of street dealers.

But just when it looked like things were going well, everything changed. The European gang he was dealing with were all arrested in a massive bust. They were importing large quantities of drugs into the country via Felixstowe docks. It meant, overnight, Harry's supply dried up.

His customers started getting restless. He needed to find an alternative supplier, and fast. Luckily, he was introduced to the Russians.

A couple of years later, he came across someone who had a unique product but no way of selling it. They needed the network of sellers that Harry had spent years building. The pair formed what turned out to be a highly lucrative partnership.

As the drugs business became more successful, Harry became more worried. He had nightmares of the police catching him and his world crashing down into tiny pieces. Ever since he'd worked on the building sites, his desire had always been to build a property empire.

Then, one night, at a charity dinner, he found himself talking to Baroness Sanjrani. She introduced Harry to Peter Hogan and Tommy Quickman. Two members of the council planning committee.

As Harry got to know these people, he soon found out they were happy to accept backhanders. In return, they offered him council-owned parcels of land at discounted prices.

He saw this as an opportunity to sell his interest in the drugs business and concentrate on building his property empire. He would be able to continue living his life of luxury without the fear of the police knocking at his door.

CHAPTER FIFTEEN

NORMAN WAKEFIELD

Monday 2nd February 2015

For the past fifty years, Wilson's petrol station has taken pride of place at 309 Woolston Road. But today, seventy-eight-year-old Ron Wilson has decided to close the business and retire. It follows a health scare and the common sense expressed by his long-suffering wife.

The closure has come as a blow to Norman Wakefield, who rents the premises to Ron. Norman also runs his own business, Wakefield Printing Works, from buildings behind the petrol station.

It's the business his father, William, started sixty years ago and built up by working seven days a week. After ten years, the business was booming. So in January 1965, when he had the opportunity to buy the freehold of the land, he decided it would be a good investment.

The two-acre site was much larger than he needed. And, back then, thirty thousand pounds was a lot of money. To help cover the mortgage, he rented the front half of the site to Ron Wilson, who opened a petrol station.

A year later, William became a proud father. The boy was christened Norman. A good traditional working-class name of the time.

One of the proudest moments for William, was when, at the age of eighteen, his son joined him in the business.

Three years later, Norman married Vivian White. And the following year, the couple were able to tell William he was to become a grandfather. They named her Diana, a popular name of the time.

When William passed away in 2002, he left everything to Norman who carried on the business. But times have changed, and now, with the petrol station closing, it means a big dip in rental income for Norman.

The situation is not helped by the fact the printing business is suffering financially. Recent advances in computers and printers means customers can produce their own stationery.

The petrol station is the main reason people visit the area. Its closure has had a huge impact on nearby shops. This includes Dave Rex's kebab takeaway, located a few doors down at number 301.

With his shop lease up for renewal, Dave has found what he considers a better location. It's about half a mile along the road, over the railway bridge and closer to the town centre.

The only problem is it doesn't have the relevant planning permission for a food outlet. He's aware several people have applied for a change of use in the last three years. Each of them had their application rejected.

Luckily for Dave, he has an ace up his sleeve and – as any poker player is aware – it helps if you know your opponents' cards.

As someone who is methodical in everything he does, Dave likes to keep tight control of the Eastern European girls in his escort agency. One of the things he does is get them to report back any interesting information their punters tell them when they are *enjoying their company between the sheets*.

Just like women will discuss their innermost secrets with a hairdresser, a punter will reveal all sorts of information to an escort, usually to *big* themselves up.

One of his girls, Rema, recently told Dave about a regular client who claims to be a big shot in the local council.

When she passed on the information, Dave checked him out. It seems it was true: according to the council website, he is the head of the planning department. Dave knows he will have a lot of influence on the local planning committee. Rema has told Dave the man is a regular punter, visiting her every Thursday evening at six thirty.

Whenever the situation requires, Dave can turn on the charm. So, the following week, he greets Rema's regular punter outside her place. He informs him she isn't feeling well, and leads him to a different apartment.

Dave knocks at the door and stands back to watch the man's reaction to meeting his top girl, Monique.

The moment forty-eight-year-old Peter Hogan sees her, his eyes widen, his mouth drops open. Comparing this blonde bombshell to Rema is like offering someone a Victoria sponge cake *personally* baked by Mary Berry when their usual treat is a budget supermarket brand.

"Monique only deals with my special clients," Dave explains, noticing the lust in Peter's eyes. He knows, after spending time with Monique, this punter will be willing to pay any price to see her again, but Dave won't be after his cash. He has something else in mind.

An hour later, Peter emerges from the apartment, totally exhausted and satisfied from head to toe. He has never known a woman with so much passion.

Dave allows Hogan two more visits with Monique before he approaches him again.

"I recently put in an application for 202 Woolston Road for use as a takeaway. I was wondering if you might be able to offer me some advice as to how to get my planning change-of-use approved." Dave remains silent about the photos taken by the camera hidden in Monique's bedroom. He'll only use them as a last resort.

Peter's raised eyebrow shows he understands the gist of Dave's request. "I suppose, given that Woolston Road is an up-and-coming area, I can have a word and get my colleagues to look at your application in a sympathetic manner."

Five weeks later, Dave received the approval he needed from the council.

He realises it would be a smart move to remain friendly with the head of the local planning department. He has a word with Monique and tells her to make sure she always offers Peter Hogan her very best VIP treatment.

CHAPTER SIXTEEN

PETER HOGAN

Monday 4th May 2015

Peter Hogan is standing at the notorious sixteenth hole on Trentbridge Golf Course. His golf partner is Baroness Sanjrani, a trained barrister. She is currently seeking re-election as secretary general of a government-funded quango, The North West England Advisory Board. Besides this, she is also a member of the local council planning committee.

"Peter, you need to find a solution to our problem. I can't afford to have these latest allegations hanging over me. Let's hope they don't go back and investigate what we did. That bloody detective – what was his name? – he just seemed to disappear. Are you sure you had nothing to do with that? If you did, perhaps you could arrange the same again?"

The episode the Baroness is referring to flashes through Peter's mind. He shudders at the thought of how close they had come to getting caught.

Five years ago, it looked like they would face criminal fraud and corruption charges.

Two disgruntled local developers had made allegations, claiming a rival had paid backhanders to purchase valuable council-owned land at discounted prices. They had approached the chairman of the council, who, in turn, called in the police, and a major investigation had got underway.

The man in charge was Detective Chief Inspector Larry Archer. He spent two months investigating the allegations.

After their close encounter, the pair kept a low profile. But the temptation of easy money proved hard to resist, and they crept back into their old dishonest ways.

A local developer offered a large cash sum in exchange for a multi-million-pound contract to build a new leisure complex.

One of the other companies who bid on the project became suspicious. They reported the details to the head of the council, who had no option but to inform the police. They are now on the verge of opening an inquiry.

The Baroness takes a practice swing, then looks around, addressing her golf partner sharply. "Peter, are you listening to me?"

Upon hearing the elevated voice of the Baroness, his thoughts return to the present.

"Look," Peter responds. "Whatever happened to that detective had nothing to do with me. If someone paid him off or was responsible for his disappearance, I have no knowledge of it. Besides, you're in politics. You must know lots of people in low places."

"Yes, but they're not the sort who like to get their hands dirty. Now be quiet, and let me concentrate while I take this shot."

The Baroness takes a swing, seems satisfied, and steps back. Peter strolls up to the tee. He pulls out his newest club, a Callaway Big Bertha iron. He lines up his shot and watches it fly.

From what he can see, it lands about ten yards from its intended target. He smiles and looks around for words of praise but instead receives a terse admonishment.

"This is serious, Peter. I've tried my best to put pressure on the police to abandon the investigation. But it's too late. The deputy chief constable informs me it's out of his hands.

"A detective has already been assigned. He's due to start work on the case at the beginning of June, which gives us three weeks. So, you better get on and sort out this little problem. Fast."

Peter looks up thoughtfully. "Wait! Maybe there is a way. I've just thought of someone I came across recently who might be able to arrange something. He's a bit of a dodgy character, and he owes me a favour. I get the feeling he's just the type of person we need."

CHAPTER SEVENTEEN

DAVE

Monday 11th May 2015

Peter Hogan and Baroness Sanjrani have invited Dave Rex for a meal at their favourite restaurant.

It isn't a place he is familiar with. The frontage looks garish from the outside with diamond-shaped graphics of gold symbols. Once inside, he finds it's a different story. The décor is still over the top, but the room has a welcoming atmosphere. There is space between the tables, not the crammed-in layout of many restaurants.

Before Dave manages three steps inside, the maître d' greets him like a long-lost friend.

"Good afternoon, sir. How are you today?"

"I'm well, thank you." Dave looks over the man's shoulder, glancing around.

"Ah. You are here to meet someone?" enquires the man, speaking with a prominent French accent.

"Yes, that's right."

"Would it be Monsieur Hogan and his guest, by some chance?"

Dave nods.

"Please, come this way."

Dave is led through to the rear of the restaurant. A garden terrace with eight booths spread around the outside and a Mediterranean garden in the centre.

In the corner booth sit the two people Dave is here to meet.

Peter Hogan stands to shake Dave's hand. The Baroness remains in her seat, sipping on what looks like a delicious cocktail.

"I'll give you some time to study the menu, then send your waiter over."

"Thank you, Angelo," Peter says.

The maître d' bows and walks away.

Once the waiter has taken their order for starters, Peter looks across to the Baroness, who nods.

"Mr Rex. We have a slight problem and wonder if you might be able to advise us on how to deal with it. As members of the local planning committee, we recently agreed to a multi-million-pound contract to build a new leisure complex. Everything above board, of course."

Dave is about to laugh but manages to hold it in. "Yes, of course."

"Anyway," says Peter.

But before he can continue, the Baroness interjects.

"Another developer, who is obviously mistaken, has told the head of the council that we accepted a bribe. He, in turn, has called in the police."

Peter looks across, waiting for her to say more. When she doesn't, he continues.

"So, we're wondering if you could help us and come up with a solution to stop the investigation. It would be most embarrassing, and we wish to prevent it."

"Yes. I completely understand your predicament," Dave replies with a hint of sarcasm. "No doubt you are totally innocent, but these things have a habit of sticking, don't they."

"Quite so," the Baroness says.

She stops speaking when the waiter appears.

"Is everything satisfactory with your meals?"

"Absolutely divine," Peter replies.

"Yes. Lovely," the Baroness adds.

"Mmmm. Delicious," Dave says.

The waiter bows and leaves.

Peter continues to explain the situation with the forthcoming police investigation.

As he sits back, the Baroness leans in, using a soft voice. "At the end of the month, they're bringing in a detective to open a new case. We need to find a way to put a stop to it."

Dave smiles. "Leave it with me. I'm sure I can find a solution."

"It would be more reassuring if we have your word that you can handle it." The Baroness's voice gives away her concern.

Dave picks up the menu. "You have my word. You can consider it done. Now, these desserts look good. What do you recommend?"

An hour later, after Dave gets home, he walks into the lounge and pours himself a large Jack Daniel's. He knows if anything happens to the detective, the police will become suspicious. They will go through all the detective's current and upcoming cases to find a motive.

Instead, he must get him *out of the way* without arousing suspicion.

It doesn't take Dave long to devise the perfect solution.

Far better if something were to happen to someone close to him. Someone the man cares about. Members of his family would be ideal. Make it look like an accident.

Dave knows two Albanians who are always prepared to undertake *removal tasks*. The price will be ten grand, but Dave will cover the cost. After all, having someone inside the council, in his debt, will be worth far more. Especially after he's seen how Peter Hogan has been able to obtain the planning permission for his takeaway business.

Dave walks over to the drinks cabinet and pours himself another Jack Daniel's. He picks up his phone and dials.

Five minutes later, he ends the call and chuckles to himself. He's just ordered the death of three people. He'll sleep well tonight.

CHAPTER EIGHTEEN

JAMES

Thursday 14th May 2015

It's a beautiful spring day, and I'm enjoying the warmth of the sun on my face. I notice that many of the flowerbeds are coming into bloom. I've spent the morning pottering around in the garden and cutting the grass. By the time I've locked the mower back in the shed, my stomach's reminding me it's close to lunchtime.

I head into the kitchen, brew coffee and make myself a cheese and pickle sandwich. I move into the lounge to catch up with the lunchtime news. I'm sad to hear that blues legend BB King has died.

I switch off the TV, dig out my *BB King & Friends* CD, and lay back on the sofa, closing my eyes. Time seems to stand still as I drift away into a world of my own. The brilliance of his guitar playing sends shivers down my spine.

Halfway through 'The Thrill Is Gone', I hear the *rat-tat-tat* of the front door knocker. I'm expecting Miriam, and the kids – Jack's now five and Abigail's three – back after visiting her parents for a few days. I assume Miriam has misplaced her keys, as she often does, or Jack has run ahead to give me a hug.

I rush to open the door, expecting to greet my family. But my smile drops when I'm confronted by a fresh-faced police officer, and a woman in her early thirties standing alongside him.

Most people would try to remember if they'd been speeding or forgotten to renew their car tax. But, as a serving police detective, I know they haven't come to discuss a minor traffic offence.

"Hello, sir. Are you James Sheldon?"

My heart is pounding, but I manage to nod. My instinct tells me something terrible has happened. "We haven't met before. I'm Carla Parsons, the new detective sergeant. I transferred yesterday from Derby. Can we step inside?"

I invite them into the lounge and notice her body tense. Then she delivers the words that will haunt me forever.

"I'm so sorry to have to tell you that your wife and two children have been involved in a fatal accident."

For a few seconds, DS Parsons says nothing. I know from my own police training that she's paused to allow the message to sink in.

Then she continues, "We're not sure of the full facts at this point. The incident happened outside the Saverland supermarket. It appears to be a hit-and-run. According to an eyewitness, there were two men. They fled the scene in a vehicle reported as stolen earlier."

The tone of her voice softens. "I'm so sorry for your loss. Is there anyone we can contact to come and be with you?"

I notice her nod to the young uniformed officer, a signal for him to go into the kitchen and start filling the kettle.

As if a cup of tea will bring them back.

The following day

I finally manage to stagger downstairs, still dressed in yesterday's attire, minus my left sock. According to the clock in the hallway, it's lunchtime. I wander into the lounge holding my aching head. I trip over the empty whisky bottles and almost break my leg.

The house is eerily quiet. It takes me a minute to register why. Then the realisation kicks in. The visit from the two police officers yesterday and the news one imparted.

Bit by bit, it all starts to come back to me. I knew there was something I needed to do today. Now I remember what it is.

I've got to arrange the funerals of my lovely wife and two beautiful children.

CHAPTER NINETEEN

JAMES

Tuesday 26th May 2015

The sun is shining from a pure blue sky. But to be honest, I would have preferred it if it had poured with rain. It would have suited the occasion better. Not that *any* weather is ideal when you're burying your family.

The main thing that comforts me is the presence of my work colleagues, here to offer their support.

I'm grateful to see DCI Gerry Payne, who has come along with his wife, Paddy. I'm also glad to see DI Phil Jones, who left the police three years ago to start his own private investigation business.

And I notice Tracy Archer, DCI Larry Archer's daughter. I'm sure he would be proud of her decision to join the force. I guess we'll never know the truth about his disappearance.

For the funeral service, the vicar does his best under the circumstances. Later in the day, as the wake drags on, I just about hold it together. Things are not helped each time someone I don't even recognise tries to offer words of comfort. I know they mean well, but to be honest, I just wish they'd all fuck off.

By seven p.m., it seems everyone has taken the hint. I'm left alone in what has become a cold empty space to face the world without the people who *were* my world. All I have are memories of when it had been a house full of joy and laughter.

I recall the time I'd taken Jack to his first football match. I wanted to make it special, so we went to Birmingham v Leicester. The game was exciting; 3–2, with the home team scoring the winning goal during injury time.

My darling little Abigail, who loved dressing up as a princess. She was a real Daddy's girl, with her golden hair and that lovely big smile like her mother's. If only she'd had the chance to grow into a teenager, I know she would have broken quite a few hearts.

In my mind, standing by my side, I see the girl of my dreams: my beautiful Miriam. From the first time I saw her, I knew she was the one. We'd been planning to have another child when the time was right. When she died, she was only thirty-three.

My bosses at Trentbridge Police have given me time off for compassionate leave. It means the investigation into local council corruption, which I was about to lead, will be put on hold. Or it could be passed on to another overworked detective. But more than likely, they'll decide to dump it into the 'not a priority' – better known as NAP – file.

All I know is that it won't be me leading the investigation. I'm too far into the bottle and slipping deeper with each passing day.

CHAPTER TWENTY

JAMES

Tuesday 12th January 2016

I don't recall much about the past eight months. They've all disappeared into a haze of booze.

The local takeaways know my order without asking, and the only time I venture past the front door is to the local corner shop to pick up my friend Johnnie Walker. I go through a bottle a day, maybe two – I lose count. I tend to lounge around the house until the alcohol numbs the pain.

Quite often, things aren't helped by the return of the migraine headaches I suffered as a child.

As for my appearance, I grab whatever's closest. My socks don't match, and I rarely bother to tuck in my shirt. The washing machine has become redundant.

One morning, at around seven thirty, I'm woken by a loud thumping on the front door. At first, I ignore it, but it seems whoever is outside isn't going away.

After several knocks, I hear the letterbox clatter, followed by a booming voice.

"Mr Sheldon. We know you're in there. Can you answer the door please? It's important we speak with you."

I stagger up from the sofa in the lounge, where I drunkenly passed out last night.

When I eventually reach the front door, I'm confronted by three burly men. The main guy informs me they're court bailiffs. He holds up an ID badge, which, in my still-drunken state, I can't focus on to read. Then he hands me a piece of paper.

"I'm sorry, Mr Sheldon, but we're here from the county court. This is an eviction order served on behalf of your mortgage company. They're repossessing the house."

I recall getting the reminders. I told myself I'd deal with them tomorrow, but that turned into the next day then the next. I guess after eight months, they've finally run out of patience.

The guy holding the paperwork looks at me sympathetically. "Look, pal. There's nothing we can do to stop it. It's the court's decision. If you take my advice, you'll grab some clothes and anything else you need and stuff it all in a suitcase. Then go and put yourself at the mercy of a friend or relative until you get things sorted. I'll give you a few minutes, but that's all I can do."

I really can't be bothered to hunt around for a suitcase and I don't want to become a burden to Miriam's parents.

So I leave 32 Langham Close with the same threads I've been wearing for a week. I'm carrying a black bag filled with the first items of clothing I manage to lay my hands on. I also make sure to grab my most precious possession: an almost-full bottle of Johnnie Walker.

As I stagger away, leaving everything I own behind me, even in my hungover state, I can feel the chill of the January air. I stumble back inside and grab my thick overcoat from the clothes peg in the hallway.

Then, as I trudge back down the path and reach the road, I notice a locksmith's van draw up. These guys know what they're doing. I realise there's no chance of me sneaking back in later when they've gone.

Being drunk before most people have finished their breakfast makes you feel indestructible. In truth, it leaves you vulnerable. I really didn't think my departure through: I left my mobile, although nobody would take my calls anyway, and I left my keyring which had the photos of those I treasure most on it.

I also left behind my dignity.

As the drink wears off, it's replaced by both fear and the reality of my situation. I'm now on the streets with nowhere to go and no address to return to.

By mid-morning, the whisky bottle is empty. The cold air makes my nose run. As I search my coat pockets for a tissue, I find a twenty-pound note and some loose change. It must be from a purchase I've long forgotten about. So, my next stop is the corner shop, where I've spent so much on booze that I should own shares in the place.

As if the day hasn't been shitty enough, I'll never forget going up to the counter while clutching a bottle of cheap whisky. I'm shocked to read the newspaper headlines telling me David Bowie has died.

With my next drink of the day, I raise my bottle to him.

RIP, Starman.

My unexpected bonus won't run to a second bottle. So, I amble towards the town centre to find a cash machine and extract some money. But it seems my bank has other ideas, as neither of my cards has been returned. All I get is a brief message, something about them needing to be retained.

And it isn't even lunchtime.

I need somewhere to think things over, so I head for the local park and a place to rest. It seems the bench must be reserved, especially for me, because no one else wants to share it.

An hour or so later, a police community support officer passes by. He's polite but firm: "I'm sorry, sir, but you can't stay here." He's probably only a few days into the job, yet here he is telling me, a former police detective, that I need to move on.

My brain takes it in: *former*. A past-tense word. I'm not sure if this is reality or a nightmare from which I will soon wake up.

Perhaps on reflection, my note telling them they could stuff their job wasn't a good move. But it's too late now.

Thoughts run around in my head: *Where can I go? How can I pass the hours? What will I do after the shops close?*

Where will I spend the night? Where can I get food? And most importantly, *where will my next drink come from?*

A few months ago, I was a respected and newly promoted detective inspector in the police. Now I'm reduced to being a down-and-out homeless drunk.

CHAPTER TWENTY-ONE

JAMES

January to May 2016

I recall when I first became homeless, I started off using hostels. I soon learned they should be called *hostiles*. The volatile nature of some of the residents can make them a more dangerous place than the outside world.

The staff try their best to check everyone coming in. But they don't have the cunning ways of the addicts and alcoholics.

Believe me, if a drug addict wants to get their stash into the hostel, nothing will stop them. Some are absolute scumbags.

In the circles of the homeless, illegal highs are in common use. Here in Trentbridge, Monkey Dust is rife. Popular because it's cheap, and it blocks out everything. And I do mean *everything*.

After my bad experiences with the hostels, I progressed – if that's the right word – to sleeping in shop doorways. You soon learn this has its downside. Especially on Friday and

Saturday nights, after the bars and clubs close. That's when you're woken abruptly by drunken louts who think nothing of urinating on you simply for the fun of it. And they're the nice ones. After the fifth kicking and punching session, I decided enough was enough.

I spent most of my time trying to work out where my next drink would come from. The world looks more bearable through the haze of alcohol.

I don't care that my health's going downhill, and my body can't take much more abuse.

I have no close relatives and no one to care about. Dad died when I was ten, and Mum passed away eight years ago. I remember the day well. It was two days after I attended the funeral of that poor girl, Elaine Turner. With my wife and kids gone, everyone I care about has been taken from me. I lost contact with Miriam's parents when I was made homeless. I heard they moved down to the south coast, but I don't have an address.

Living seems the worst option of the two. I'm alone in the world. I really have nothing left. So what's the point?

Over the past three weeks, I've begged hard and saved every penny.

I now have forty-two pounds.

Enough to buy one gramme of cocaine. Enough to help me join my loved ones.

I've never used drugs. I know my body won't be able to deal with the sudden surge, and one dose will be fatal.

I guess it's time to admit that my luck has run out.

So, it's going to be goodbye cruel world.

CHAPTER TWENTY-TWO

GERRY PAYNE

Friday 19th February 2016

DCI Gerry Payne turns the key and steps through his front door after a particularly tough day. He doesn't usually bring his work home; it's too depressing. But there's another matter – one he *can* discuss. He plonks down in his favourite armchair and pours out his frustration to his wife.

"I don't know why I bother. Six hours spent in a meeting on health and safety. They expect us to go out and face all sorts of hardened criminals and little shits who carry knives and even guns. Yet now they've got me going around the department checking the fire extinguishers and making sure none of the doorways are blocked. I'm supposed to be a bloody senior detective. I almost told the ACC where he can stick his job. I've bloody had enough."

His wife, Paddy, moves behind his chair and massages his shoulders. "In that case, you might be interested in something I found out at work today; you know we do the accounts for the Fenton Motel, right?"

She doesn't wait for a response.

"Well, the people who have owned it for the past thirty-two years have decided to retire. They want to sell the business."

Paddy pushes her thumbs down into her husband's shoulder blades, just the way he likes it. "I've had a word with them, and they've told me how much they want for it. As I do the bookkeeping for their accounts, I know it makes a good profit, and that's despite the owners having let things slide because they're both in their late seventies. If we were to take it over, I'm certain we could make a real go of it. It has massive potential. What do you think?"

"I'll tell you what I think."

Paddy's shoulders draw up as if steeling herself for an argument. She's aware his job has always been everything. Gerry joined the police when he was twenty-one and has worked his way up to DCI.

"I think," he continues, "it's probably the best idea I've heard in years. After today, I've had it. I've put in my thirty years. I'll get the full pension. Call these people and tell them we'll buy it."

Paddy gasps. "Are you certain? You won't change your mind tomorrow?"

"No, darling. I've been thinking about getting out for a while. I've given my best years to the job, been a good honest copper, and got little thanks in return. This sounds like the perfect opportunity. Now, what's for tea? I'm bloody starving."

Gerry has witnessed his job change over recent years. Instead of investigative work, he now has to deal with unnecessary internal paperwork and meeting targets and budgets.

The pair sit to eat.

"What's made you change your mind?" Paddy asks.

"Some days, I feel more like a glorified office manager than a detective. And the introduction of so-called local police and crime commissioners hasn't helped. What these people know about policing wouldn't fill a postcard. Every police officer knows these are politically motivated idiots on a six-figure salary, while high-ranking detectives are paid less than half that. And to make matters worse, they bring in their mates as their deputy on a salary of eighty thousand a year. It's a joke."

Gerry is one of the few long-serving officers to remain happily married. Both Gerry and Paddy's parents passed away in recent years. They inherited their houses, which they currently rent out. Their four children are grown up and have set up homes of their own.

Paddy stands and goes over to the sideboard and brings back a sheet of paper. "I've done some calculations. If we sell this house, plus the two we currently rent out, we'll have enough to buy the freehold. And your pension will help tide us over as we build up the business."

"Sounds good to me. Are you okay to sell off your parents' old house?"

"They'd understand. How about you? It's where you grew up."

"Lovely memories, but we need to look to the future."

"The money we get from them will ensure we don't have to borrow from the bank."

Gerry gives his wife a big grin. "That's my girl. Once a bookkeeper..."

CHAPTER TWENTY-THREE

JAMES SHELDON/STEVIE EVANS

Saturday 14th May 2016

One of the so-called luxuries of being on the streets is the amount of spare time you have.

And there's a question I've asked myself many times to pass the hours. How many people will the average person meet during their lifetime? In the end, I estimate it could be anywhere between two and ten thousand.

And out of all these people, perhaps twenty will become friends. And, if you're lucky, you'll have at least a handful of *real* friends. However, you only ever have one *best* friend.

When Miriam was killed, I lost my best friend. I never thought I'd find anyone else to share my thoughts and feelings with again.

I'm standing in St Matthew's Church for two reasons: the first is to get out of the thrashing rain for five minutes, and the second is to ask God to forgive me for what I'm about to do.

Last night, I exchanged the forty-two pounds. The item I scored is sitting in a wrap in my coat pocket.

I'm standing behind the pews at the back of the church when I hear a lovely thick Welsh accent behind me.

"A'right. 'Ow's it goin'? I'm Stevie, Stevie Evans." He holds out his hand to shake mine.

I take it reluctantly, but one look at his warm smile draws me in. "Hi. James Sheldon. Nice to meet you, Stevie," I reply with little in the way of enthusiasm. He doesn't seem to notice.

"Are you sheltering from the rain, or here, like me, hoping your prayers will be answered?"

"I... I, er, I guess I'm asking for forgiveness," I try to explain. I don't want to tell anyone what I'm planning to do, but this man has something about him that I instantly warm to. His manner makes it seem like he actually cares. I can see he's waiting for me to say more.

"The truth is, life has lost its meaning. I've got nothing left to live for."

"You have yourself. *You* are worth living for. It may be raining outside, but give it time, and things will brighten up. Life is *so* precious. We're about the same age. Some people don't even make it this far. Yesterday has gone. All that matters is right now."

At this point, I break down in tears.

Two people walk in so Stevie guides me over to a quiet corner and asks me what's wrong.

Without meaning to, I spurt out all about my wife and two kids. What I don't tell him is that today marks the first anniversary of their deaths. I guess he sees the signs of a man on the edge, and wants to help.

He wraps his arms around my chest and gives me a hug,

which comes as a shock. Physical contact with another human being means everything. And, at this exact moment, I swear the spot where we're standing becomes illuminated by a beam of bright light. Maybe it's the sun bursting through the clouds. Who knows?

Without Stevie, there's no way I could have coped, and I'd be on my way to a dark alleyway to end it all. Now, all I know is that my outlook on life has changed drastically.

Over the following days and weeks, Stevie's care and genuine friendship offers me the support I need. He's put his own life on hold and devoted his time to making sure I'm all right.

Whenever I turn round, he's there, not because he needs to be, but because he cares. We've made a genuine connection.

He sees things in me that I've never seen in myself. I hope I can return the favour one day.

Stevie is one of those rare people who always sees the positive side. He's taught me that life is precious, no matter where you find yourself or how bad things look at the time.

With his help, I've learned to be more positive. His genuine kindness and understanding are helping me overcome the ghosts of my past.

Gradually, the black turns to grey, and, little by little, the world comes back into focus. Before I met Stevie, I didn't have a future, but now, whatever happens, I know I want to be part of it.

Maybe my luck has changed for the better because he's the best friend anyone could ever wish for.

Stevie is a good-natured, proud Welshman with a big

heart. He moved to Trentbridge to find work because of the high level of unemployment in his hometown. Living with his parents caused friction, which led to heated rows. After deeply cutting words were exchanged, Stevie decided the best option was to move out of the area.

He took the first job he could find, and things were looking good. Then he realised his shift manager and another work colleague were stealing from the warehouse. He reported them to the branch boss but they rejected his claim, which resulted in him losing his job and ending up on the streets.

He keeps in touch with his mum via a weekly phone call.

Thankfully, it seems they've settled most of their differences.

I thank God for bringing Stevie into my life. He truly is one in a million.

CHAPTER TWENTY-FOUR

JAMES

May 2016

The month of May can be unpredictable. Some nights are warm, but there are plenty when even a brass monkey would be worried.

Using what I thought were long-forgotten detective skills, I've found a secluded spot behind the Albion, a four-star hotel. The front entrance is on Shaw Street, but I've found a sheltered area down an alleyway near the Dean Street entrance at the back. I'm hoping Stevie and I can use it as a place to bed down if we're discreet and don't draw attention to ourselves.

It looks secure, and if we keep out of the way during the day, I'm pretty sure no one will notice us. All we want is somewhere safe to get some shut-eye.

Tonight's our first night. We arrive at eight thirty with our meagre possessions, such as they are. We're about to lay out our blankets when a man strolls out of the back entrance to light up a cigarette. His uniform indicates he works there.

He glances over at us. I decide the best thing is to say something. "We're not here to cause any trouble. We only want a safe place to sleep. We'll be out of your way early in the morning."

"Hey, it's fine," he replies in a gentle reassuring voice.

He offers us a cigarette, which we both decline.

"As long as you're not still here when the general manager arrives in the morning, and you don't leave a mess, that's fine. I've no problem with you being here."

"Thanks, mate," says Stevie.

The man just smiles and reiterates, "It's fine."

Over time, we get to know the man a little better. His name is George Leeman, and he's the night porter. He's around mid-forties.

The way he looks after us makes him a gentleman in every sense of the word. During our brief conversations, he tells us that a few years ago, he found himself in the same position. He'd lost his job and fell into debt. Finally, he had his house repossessed.

So he knows what it's like. Fortunately, his brother took him in and helped him to get back on his feet.

Once or twice a week, we find a small bag of tasty left-overs from the kitchen. Little deeds like this mean a lot.

Other people might know it as the Albion Hotel. But, because of George and one or two other kind members of staff, I've given it the moniker of 'The Ritz'. After all, compared to the shop doorways and hostels I've been used to, it's five-star accommodation.

George works a ten-hour shift five nights a week, from eight until six. He usually takes his cigarette breaks on the other side of the hotel. But from time to time, he comes out and makes sure we're all right.

Over the following weeks, we manage to chat with one of the other hotel employees: a young man called Freddie, who often comes outside for a crafty cigarette. He shows us a place to store our sleeping bags rather than carry them around all day.

Compared to most people living on the streets, Stevie and I have it easy. But I wouldn't wish even that on anyone.

CHAPTER TWENTY-FIVE

JAMES

Wednesday 3rd August 2016

Yesterday, Stevie gave me some bad news: he's moving back to Rhyl to look after his mother, who's been taken ill.

I'm sure he could have gone sooner, but he stuck around until he felt confident that I wouldn't do anything stupid.

That's typical of Stevie, always putting other people first.

Naturally, I'm sad to see him go, but, on the other hand, I understand. There's nothing like having a loving family.

Every Wednesday morning, between eight and nine, I try to sneak into Hartwell's Hostel. If I can, I make use of their shower and washroom facilities.

I always try to time it for when the staff are changing shifts and busy. That way, I can be in and out in half an hour, and no one's any the wiser. They request that their residents leave by nine thirty. It's mainly a group of ten regulars: eight men and two women who spend all day chatting and drinking.

They tend to congregate around a couple of wooden benches on a large roundabout. It's right in the centre of an area called Kirby's Junction. From time to time, they wander off and buy cans of beer from the small shop run by Mr Miah and his wife.

The name Kirby's comes from a ladies' and gents' clothing store that opened in 1902. It dominated the area until it closed in 1992. After that, it became a discount store. Then, three years ago, the council installed parking restrictions, making it virtually impossible for customers to park. As a result, the business closed down, and the premises have been vacant ever since.

CHAPTER TWENTY-SIX

DAVE

Tuesday 9th August 2016

Since Dave started following Mohammad's advice and invested in local businesses, his lifestyle has been transformed. He has no desire to go back to his old one.

Thanks to Dave's attention to detail, each of the businesses he's purchased has gone from being a loss maker to making a reasonable profit. But they make a whole lot more after the extra money Dave pumps in from his drugs business.

The result has been to transform his image. He's gone from a 'Dodgy Dave' character into Dave Rex, the successful local entrepreneur. He's even been elected chairman of the Trentbridge small-business association.

It's in his nature to be organised and methodical; he likes to keep control of things.

Dave uses the services of the accountant Mohammad recommended. It means he pays his tax and VAT, and enjoys an executive income that looks totally legitimate.

It has enabled him to buy a luxury villa in Spain, drive a top-of-the-range Mercedes, and wear fine clothes and expensive watches.

His illegal income has grown substantially, but he's not convinced that buying more businesses is the best solution. In his opinion, trying to hide the cash coming from his drugs business by putting it through his so-called *legit* businesses is a clumsy way to run things.

He's worried that the profits look too good to be true. If the authorities start to look into his business empire, they might be able to work out that it's not possible for them to make the level of income he is claiming.

Last night, he had a nightmare that left him shaking. He was standing in front of the same judge who had previously given him a suspended sentence.

"David Alan Rex. You have been found guilty, and I hereby sentence you to twenty years. I hope you enjoy prison food and being locked in your tiny cell. Take him down."

His alarm clock goes off.

It's the second time in the past week he's woken up lying on bed sheets covered in sweat.

Each time, he jumped in the shower, trying to make sense of it. In the end, he's decided it's a sign.

So, what he's looking for is the same level of income but without the risk.

Surely other drug dealers must have come up against the same problem. He recalls what Vladimir said about the man they used to deal with in Trentbridge years ago. The Russian mentioned that he moved into the property business.

Dave decides it would be wise to ask the Russian for his thoughts on the matter.

But before he can deal with that, Dave receives a phone call that gets him very excited. It's from the guy who runs the Strand Vinyl Record Store. Would Dave be interested in some of the discs from the large collection of rare jazz records they've just acquired? Dave heads straight down to the shop, and, much to the delight of the owner, he purchases the lot.

Now he's sitting in his lounge, literally drooling over the disc in his hands. He lifts it to his nose and breathes in the smell of the vinyl. It's a record he's been desperately hoping to find for over three years.

A near-mint copy of *The Bird Blows the Blues* by Charlie "Bird" Parker on the original Dial record label.

He spends the rest of the morning arranging the collection of discs into alphabetical order on the shelves in his lounge. He's looking forward to playing some of them later.

With his vinyl collection all sorted, he turns his attention to business.

He pours a generous measure of Jack Daniel's and sets it down on the round coaster sitting on his office desk.

He unlocks the top drawer and takes out the pay-as-you-go mobile that will be exchanged at his next meeting with the Russians, pre-programmed with just one number.

When the call is answered, Dave asks, "Have I got the right number for Kazan Imports? This is Dave Rex."

"David, it's nice to hear from you." He recognises Vladimir's voice. "So, my good friend, how can I help you?"

Dave tells him about his growing mountain of cash and

recurring nightmares. He explains that he doesn't want to continue buying more businesses as a front; he thinks it's too risky.

"It's good to know you are thinking this way," Vladimir says. "We have watched you grow and can see you are ready to move to the next level."

The remark catches Dave off guard, but he lets it go.

Vladimir continues. "So please tell me. How much do you have in the bank, how much in cash, and what do you have in the way of assets?"

"I've siphoned half a million through my legitimate businesses and paid tax on it. I have a further one and a half million in cash stashed away. As to assets, I've got my apartment with a small mortgage, and there's a villa in Spain."

Dave listens intently as the Russian explains, "We deal with a lot of people in a similar situation, and I'll offer you the same advice: invest in property. You should consider attending property auctions. Buying them one at a time can be time-consuming and costs more money. Or find a developer who is having cash-flow problems.

"You won't be able to use your hidden cash, but that is not a problem. We know you are someone who can be trusted. When you find the right properties, we can introduce you to one of our financial partners. They will happily offer you whatever you need at a reasonable interest rate. It will all look legitimate to the authorities.

"With the money you have in the bank and your assets, and putting your businesses up as security, we would be prepared to loan you up to fifteen million.

"We have a system where you can repay the loan using the cash you are generating. Of course, we must charge a fee for this service."

The two men chat for a further ten minutes before the call ends, with Dave thanking Vladimir for his advice.

Dave puts the phone back into his desk drawer and locks it. He picks up his personal phone and makes a call.

"Hello, Mum. How are you?"

"I'm fine, Son."

Dave smiles. "As I mentioned, I'll be going to my villa a few days before your birthday. Are you sure you don't want to come with me?"

"No thanks. At my age, I don't want the upheaval. And besides, I don't like the heat."

"There's such a thing as air-conditioning, you know."

"No. You go off and enjoy yourself, and you can take me for a meal when you get back."

"I'll pop in and see you before I go."

"Okay. But don't worry. I've got everything I need."

Dave finishes the call. Although he *does* worry about his mum, he knows she hasn't lost any of her faculties, even at the ripe old age of seventy-nine.

His chat with the Russian has him excited about the future. He sets his mind on the subject of property. There are two people he wants to speak with to get some further advice.

CHAPTER TWENTY-SEVEN

PETER

Thursday 11th August 2016

Peter Hogan stands in front of the hallway mirror. This morning, he has decided on the dark blue tie with little white stars. He thinks it looks good with his new light-blue shirt and makes him appear younger. This evening, he's meeting someone he wants to impress. Once he is happy with the way the tie looks, he calls out.

"I've got the usual Thursday evening council meeting tonight. I should be home around eight."

His wife walks through from the kitchen, takes one look, and, much to his annoyance, adjusts his tie. "There. That looks better. Eight, you say?"

"Yes, you know how the committee members love to go on."

"Okay. I'll have the food ready for then. I'm planning a steak dinner. Why don't you stop at the off-licence on the way home and choose a nice red?"

Their lips touch briefly. "Sounds like a good idea." Peter

walks out to his car. He uses the vanity mirror to adjust his tie back to the way it was.

Fifteen minutes later, he drives into the underground car park at the council's offices. He parks in his usual spot that reads, 'Reserved for Head of Planning'. He glances at the clock on the dashboard and notes the time as eight fifty-five a.m.

Cynthia glances up as her boss enters the office.

"Good morning, Peter." She leans across the desk as he walks past and hands over a copy of his daily itinerary. "Oh, and one of the councillors wants a quick word. I've written his extension number on the note for you."

"Thank you, Cynthia."

"Cup of coffee?"

"Yes, please, and I think it's going to be one of those days. Add a couple of sugars, will you?"

"Tut-tut."

"I know, I know, but I've got committee meetings all afternoon. I need something to keep me awake." Peter walks through to his office.

Three and a half hours later, Cynthia knocks and pops her head around the door. "Peter, just to remind you, the meeting starts in half an hour."

"Thanks, Cynthia."

Today's meeting is to discuss ways to find thirty million pounds. That's the amount they need to cover shortfalls within the council budget. They blame the lack of funding on central government. No matter how much they receive, it never seems to be enough.

It's not a situation unique to Trentbridge.

The city of Liverpool has six thousand empty houses and has started a scheme. They plan to sell the ones in the worst state of repair for one pound each. The project is called 'Homes for a Pound'. Of course, it isn't long before unscrupulous people are finding ways to take advantage.

And it isn't only the houses. The mayor of Liverpool is currently under police investigation. He is facing charges of conspiracy, bribery, and witness intimidation. It's all to do with awarding development contracts in return for backhanders.

So, Trentbridge is far from the only town where under-the-counter deals are done.

After the council chairman gives his opening words, followed by the heads of various departments giving long-winded speeches, it's Peter's turn to address the council bigwigs.

"I've looked at the proposals put forward, and there are several properties and parcels of land that could be sold off. I estimate these should raise the amount we need. You should each have a copy of the list I've prepared.

"There's a valuable plot of land, suitable for redevelopment, at the junction of Kirby Street and Elder Road; a twenty-one thousand-square-foot industrial warehouse unit alongside the A500; the old school premises on Clare Road; a good-sized plot on Lockwood Road; and the old fire station premises on Turnock Street. Then there's the question of

Asbury Park. I think we can all agree that if this could be sold off, it would save us a great deal of money. I know we've tried to offload it in the past, but I suggest we lower the price and see what bids, if any, come in?"

Peter looks around the table. Two of the members look like they are asleep. He doesn't think his speech has been that boring. It's more than likely down to the sumptuous five-course lunch they enjoyed earlier. He sits, and the chairman stands.

"Thank you for that, Peter. Does anyone have any questions about the proposed sell-off of these sites?" He glances around the table; no one replies.

"In that case, I'll have the council lawyers start to put the paperwork together. If there are no objections, we'll set the next meeting for two weeks to announce the sale. We can then set the deadline for sealed bids for the last day of November.

"It's now four o'clock. I suggest we break for coffee and resume in thirty minutes then move on to the other matters at hand."

The meeting will probably go on until six p.m., which suits Peter fine. He can then go to his 'early-evening appointment'. The one he's dressed up for. He just hopes the person he's meeting will be wearing far less clothes than him.

An image of her comes into his mind. Sadly, *that* meeting will only last for an hour, leaving him enough time to be home for eight. He reminds himself he will need to make a stop at the off-licence.

CHAPTER TWENTY-EIGHT

DAVE

Tuesday 16th August 2016

It's been a week since Dave Rex received advice from the Russian drugs boss about buying property.

Today, along with his right-hand man Kenny, he's having one of his regular meetings with Mohammad Awan.

They're sitting at a table at the rear of Mohammad's brother's restaurant – reserved for them and out of earshot of the other customers of this busy eatery.

The waiter comes over.

"So, Sharnaz, what do you recommend today?" Dave asks.

"The Kashmiri lamb rogan is popular at the moment."

"Then I'll go for that. How about you, Kenny?"

"Sounds good."

Mohammad looks up from the menu. "The monkfish jhol for me."

After enjoying their meal, the three men walk back to the private office behind the kitchens.

As usual, Kenny picks up the large package covered in birthday wrapping paper. He takes it out to his car, places it in the boot and covers it with a blanket. He then starts the journey back to Trentbridge.

Dave stays behind to hand over the cash and discuss some business matters. He considers Mohammad to be one of the very few people he admires and can call a friend.

"So, Mohammad, I want to ask you about something you've mentioned in the past, about moving out of the drug business before the police get wise to you. I've followed your previous advice with great success. So, can you advise me on how to reach the next level?"

"I'm more than happy to help you, my friend. The business we are in has been good. But we both know that there are risks involved and, like all good things, it will come to an end. One day there could come a knock at the door from the police.

"So, I'm making plans to move on. But bear in mind, I've been in this business longer than you. It will take a while, but a few years from now, you should start to think about retiring to a nice sunny beach. To this end, I've already started investing in property.

"After all, especially around the area in London where I live, lack of housing is the main issue. They can't make any more land, so the prices keep going up and up. So, for people like us with spare cash to invest, that's great news. With high property prices, people can't afford to buy, so they must rent."

Mohammad takes a sip of his tea then continues. "Property is a solid investment, and it's the best way to hide money. Just look at the Russian oligarchs. They have billions invested in the London property market.

"My brother and I have recently closed a deal to buy ten properties here in Birmingham. We already have tenants lined up for all of them at three hundred pounds a week rental."

Dave is impressed. "Congratulations, Mohammad. That sounds like a big step forward in your retirement plan."

"Yes, we are very excited at the prospect. I have certain contacts in London who have access to thousands of tenants. So, our biggest problem is finding the properties."

Dave's eyes widen. "Can I ask? How does that work?"

Mohammad stands and walks over to a nearby desk. He picks up a manila file, pulls a cutting from *The Guardian* newspaper, and hands it to Dave.

The headline reads: 'Benefit Caps – A Disgraceful Policy That's About to Get Worse'.

It explains how the government has reduced the budgets to local councils in London: money to cover the cost of housing for families on low incomes or unemployed.

The article goes on to say the current maximum amount of housing benefit in London is set at three hundred and forty pounds a week. It mentions that Camden Council in North London has started moving families out to places as far away as Birmingham and Bradford in a bid to save money. It means private landlords can make a small fortune offering substandard housing.

Finishing the article, Dave looks across the table.

"What it means," Mohammad explains, after taking another sip of tea, "is that local councils will be forced to move tenants out of London. I have contacts within various council housing departments. For a small financial consideration, they will arrange for their councils to pay me three hundred pounds a week for each family. Over the next twelve months, they will have several thousand tenants they need to rehouse."

Mohammad gives Dave a wide grin. "My brother and I are buying the most run-down properties. All we need to do is make basic repairs. And we don't have to worry about the living conditions. The councils in London haven't got the manpower to send anyone all the way up here to inspect the properties. The local councils won't get involved because these people are not their tenants, so it's not their problem. It means we should be able to make our investment back in three or four years. That's my retirement plan.

"So, Dave, if you can find cheap properties in your area, I can introduce you to my contacts in London. These are the people who control budgets within several council housing departments. When the time comes, they would be prepared to rehouse families in Trentbridge.

"You can charge three hundred pounds a week rent for each family. Of course, there needs to be a consultancy fee for my associates and myself. Ten per cent of the weekly rental income is fair."

Mohammad sits back, looking smug.

"I tell you, Dave, this is a golden opportunity to make a fortune legally. No more looking over your shoulder or worrying about the police knocking on your front door in the middle of the night."

Dave's thoughts turn to his recent nightmares. The idea of getting a peaceful night's sleep and not having to worry about the police makes him feel better. Yes, getting into property is definitely the way to go, and he knows someone in a position to help him. Someone just as crooked as him.

CHAPTER TWENTY-NINE

DAVE

Wednesday 17th August 2016

All fired up after his meeting with Mohammad, Dave calls Peter Hogan. "Peter, I wonder if you fancy a day at the races? I've got a horse running at Chester in a couple of days. And I have a matter I'd like to discuss with you. I think it could be worth your while. We could travel up and discuss everything over a nice meal in my private box. Who knows, we might even win a few quid."

"Thanks, Dave, that sounds like fun. I do love an occasional flutter."

The two men are seated in Dave's private box, with a clear view of the racetrack. The waitress has left, saying she hopes they enjoy their food.

"Peter, I'll come to the point. I'm looking to get into the property market in a big way. Not just a couple of houses.

I'm in the market to buy a large number of properties at once. Maybe something like an entire block of apartments. Money's no object."

"You could be in luck, Dave. Like most councils, our cash reserves always seem to come up short. We had a meeting about it recently. The committee have voted to sell off some of their property assets: several major buildings, along with a few parcels of land and a semi-derelict housing estate. They're planning to make an announcement in the next few days for anyone interested to submit sealed bids: highest bid on each lot gets it, subject to final approval from the committee."

"Ideally, I'm after some cheap run-down properties," says Dave.

"In that case, the Asbury Park estate would be perfect. But it's big. I mean *big*, and it won't be cheap."

"How not cheap are we talking?"

"The location will put off most developers, being on the wrong side of the river. The properties are all in need of repairs, but we're talking about eight hundred and eighty houses. Ten million would be my guess."

Dave does a quick calculation in his head.

Eight hundred and eighty multiplied by three hundred pounds.

He can't believe it. He double-checks. It comes out the same. More than a quarter of a million a week. That means he'll recoup the entire investment in less than a year. He'll even be able to cover the interest on the loan from the Russians.

Dave finds it almost impossible not to grin. "Peter, if you can help me pull this off for that price, I'll give you a quarter of a million in cash."

Peter almost chokes on his food. "If you're sure you can come up with the money, I promise I'll do everything I can for you, Dave. But we're talking ten million."

"Believe me, Peter, that level of money is not a problem."

A week later, the council make their public announcement. They publish a list of the various properties and parcels of land, just as Peter said.

Dave's mobile rings, and he sees the caller is Peter Hogan.

"Hello, Dave. Just to let you know, the council have set the minimum bids on each property. As I suspected, for Asbury Park, it's ten million. If you bid at that level, you should be the winner. If anyone else shows any interest, I can let you know. But from what I can see, you'll have a clear field on this one."

CHAPTER THIRTY

PETER AND HARRY

Monday 5th September 2016

Peter Hogan receives a call.

"Hi, Peter, it's Harry Richardson. How are you?"

"Hello, Harry, I'm fine. Gosh, it's been a while. What can I do for you?"

"I see the council's selling off Asbury Park. I've seen the price. Looks like a sweet deal, so I thought I'd ask you about it."

"Sure, Harry. I have to warn you. It's very run-down and will cost a fortune to put right. Look, I'll be honest. I've got someone else lined up for it, and besides, it would be difficult to do anything on the price. But, tell you what. There's the old school property on Clare Road; it's ripe for redevelopment. I could work something out on that. I think you'd make more from that than you would Asbury Park, and with far less headaches."

"Do you mean the one next to Mitten's old vehicle workshop?"

"Yes. That's the one. Don't tell me you own that."

"Er, no. No. Now tell me more about what you can offer me. It sounds interesting."

Peter tells Harry he can work something out so he can get the property for half its actual value. The pair go back a long way. They were doing underhand deals six years ago until a rival developer got wind and reported them. Luckily, the police investigation came to nothing. And Peter knows Harry can't resist the temptation of an illegal deal.

At the back of his mind, Peter knows that since Harry has taken the trouble of getting in touch, he'll need to come up with a deal to keep him sweet.

Even if only half the stories he's heard are true, Harry Richardson is not someone you want to get on the wrong side of.

CHAPTER THIRTY-ONE

JAMES

Thursday 1st September 2016

I hear the distant chimes of the clock from St Matthew's Church announce ten p.m. If I leave now, I can make it to Festival Park, where I'll find the charity tea stall. Usually, three volunteers are there – come rain, shine, snow, or gale. They give up their time for free – yet take abuse, get spat at (or even worse) for no good reason.

Most nights, the Reverend Wendall Bates will be standing around. He's always ready to offer support to anyone who needs it. He never judges people. He simply listens and helps when he can. God bless him and his team.

There's the usual mix of takers when I arrive, and many more will arrive before they shut in a couple of hours. I count fourteen of us. This includes the Two Ronnies, so called because they're always together, and one's a lot shorter than the other; neither is called Ronnie. I don't know the taller one's name, but the other is Fergus McShane. He's a Glaswegian with a drinking problem – the problem is that he won't stop drinking until his liver collapses.

I take my place in the queue and wait for my turn to get a cup of tea and some hot food. I try to avoid conversation, which is difficult when people are all fired up on drinks or illegal substances.

"Can yer spare a ciggie?" asks the person I know as Young Ned. He's here with his dog, Buddy. They go everywhere together.

"Sorry, I don't smoke," I say. He's asked me the same question on numerous occasions. That's usually when he's spaced out on Monkey Dust. It's powerful and messes with your short-term memory. Just one hit of the stuff, and that's your whole day gone, vanished, for less than a fiver. That's probably the reason he takes it.

After I drain the last dregs of my tea, I offer a soft thank you to the people behind the counter. I start my journey back to the Ritz.

I'm anxious to avoid the teenage louts who come out of the bars and clubs into the night air after a few too many drinks. Some like nothing more than to take their frustrations out on anyone in sight.

I've had a couple of beatings from them in the past. They're fuelled by cheap alcohol deals and don't care who they fight or how much damage they inflict.

They'd gladly kick your head in without giving it a second thought. Just so they can post it on social media and send it to their friends, saying, 'Look what I've done'.

Thankfully, as today is a Tuesday, my luck holds out, and the streets are pretty empty. Fridays and Saturdays are the nights to avoid.

Walking past one of the shops, I catch my reflection in

the large window. I notice the change in myself. I used to weigh twelve stone; now I'd guess I'm around ten. My belt's moved in three notches. And recently, my teeth have started to hurt.

When I arrive back, I find my 'bed linen' – a sleeping bag and a blanket – have been washed, dried and returned. This happens every couple of weeks. George never talks about it, and when I try to thank him, he shrugs it off.

Since getting to know George a little better, two wooden pallets and a single mattress have also *magically* appeared. I'm so grateful to him. I may be homeless, but compared to a lot of people, I've got it easy.

You've probably never given it a thought, but undertakers get a large percentage of their business from hostels. Life expectancy is much shorter when you're homeless, especially for those who turn to alcohol or drugs to escape the harsh reality. Homeless people also have to cope with heart conditions and malnutrition. And let's not even get onto the psychological issues.

I guess this is part of my problem. Deep down inside, I feel the guilt that it was my fault. I wasn't there to save my family from the hit-and-run driver, so I deserve to live on the streets.

CHAPTER THIRTY-TWO

PETER

Friday 9th September 2016

Peter Hogan has told his wife that he's going away on a weekend management course on behalf of the council. In truth, he's booked a luxury hotel for himself and Monique.

The couple are lying in bed, sipping champagne. They're discussing the possibility of him leaving his wife and the pair setting up a home together. But the problem is, he'll need a lot of cash. Monique likes nice things, and a divorce will be messy.

So far, he's paid for various designer dresses, Chanel perfume, skimpy lingerie, two pairs of Christian Louboutin shoes and a gold necklace. He's even splashed out and bought her a car. But she's worth it. She makes him feel alive and young again. He's just hoping his wife doesn't check the family savings account and notice the thirty thousand pounds he has *borrowed* from it.

Ever since Dave introduced them, Peter thinks about Monique day and night. The woman has more passion in her little finger than his wife has in her entire body. They have talked about starting a family after they are married. And Monique promised that, at that point, she would give up seeing other men. She has told him she always thinks of him when she is with anyone else.

Peter and his wife are unable to have children, but perhaps it isn't too late for him. Once the divorce is through and he marries Monique, they can start planning.

All Peter needs is a nice chunk of cash, and thankfully he's kept Dave Rex sweet. It seems the man has more money than Peter initially realised. If Dave can afford to pay ten million for Asbury Park, there could be more deals in the future.

Perhaps he can persuade Dave to take him on as a business partner. Then he will have enough money to support Monique with a luxury lifestyle.

CHAPTER THIRTY-THREE

DAVE

Wednesday 12th October 2016

Dave Rex is celebrating his fiftieth birthday. At breakfast, his present to himself is a Montblanc Miles Davis Limited Edition 1926 rollerball pen. Dave isn't a computer person.

He drives over to spend an hour in the gym, followed by a relaxing massage. Then a visit to his favourite restaurant with his dear old mum. She prefers lunch to an evening meal.

It's a Wednesday and she doesn't like to miss the latest episode of *Coronation Street*.

"Happy birthday, Son."

"Thanks, Mum. It'll be *your* birthday soon. Your eightieth, I haven't forgotten."

"Don't remind me."

"You've got a good few years left yet." Dave is interrupted by the waiter uncorking the bottle of champagne.

"Cheers, Son. It's a shame your dad isn't here to see how well you've done. He'd have been proud."

"Cheers, Mum. Yes, I hope he would."

Reggie *'the rat'* Rex had always been skinny. And he had a particular skill. He could bend his body like a contortionist. His ability to squeeze through small spaces and climb drain-pipes had gained him his nickname.

Reggie and Dave started robbing posh apartment blocks. Reggie would scamper up the outside of a building. This way, he would avoid the CCTV covering the entrance and hallways. He would either scoop up the valuables and lower the 'bag of swag' down a rope to Dave, who would be waiting below. Or use the entry buzzer to let him into the building.

Sadly, it came to an end when Reggie was climbing a loose drainpipe on the third floor of a posh apartment block. The pipe gave way. It seems the builders were a bunch of cowboys and hadn't fastened it correctly. Reggie fell headfirst to the ground.

After his father's death, Dave moved into selling dodgy motors.

That led to another business enterprise. Setting fire to business premises while the owner gave themselves a solid alibi by being in a busy location a hundred miles away. This made it easy for them to collect on the insurance.

One of the people Dave met was Mr Ahmed, who had contacts in various overseas factories and was importing container loads of fake designer clothes.

Dave decided it looked like a winner and started selling the clothes around local pubs, until one by one, they banned him. So he set up selling on weekend markets.

It paid the bills, but he wasn't making a fortune. All the time looking for the next big thing.

Since those days, Dave has come a long way. And he's acquired a taste for the good life. He loves to wear bespoke suits, crisp white shirts, and handmade Italian shoes. He also enjoys the feel of an eighteen-carat Rolex on his wrist.

He is a season ticket holder for his local football club and a member of various golf clubs. He enjoys regular sea cruises and trips to his villa in Spain.

Dave is not a tall man, but the fruits of good living have expanded his waistline to forty inches. His weight is currently around seventeen stones. His doctor has informed him this is the cause of his high blood pressure.

In the afternoon, Dave spends an hour in the company of one of his escorts. Then a visit to his tailor to be measured up for a new suit.

"Life must be treating you well, Mr Rex. I think it would be wise if we add an extra inch to the waist this time."

Dave spends the evening at home in the company of a bottle of Jack Daniel's Sinatra Select. He pours a measure into his new personalised whisky tumbler. He sits back on his Italian white leather sofa, closes his eyes, and enjoys the burn from his first sip.

He sinks contentedly into the soft leather without a care in the world. From the stereo playing in the background, 'Bird' is giving a masterclass in jazz saxophone.

CHAPTER THIRTY-FOUR

JAMES

Tuesday 18th October 2016

It's a bitterly cold afternoon; I can feel the icy wind biting harder with each fading minute of daylight.

I'm hunched in a grubby doorway next to a 'Shop to Let' sign. On the pavement in front of me is my woolly green hat. It's sitting next to a crudely written cardboard sign that reads, 'Homeless, Please Help'.

I'm desperately hoping someone will donate a coin or two because all I have to show for the past three hours is the pitiful sum of eighty pence.

More out of hope than expectation, as people walk past, I ask, "Spare some change, please?" But they all pretend not to hear and keep walking.

What's this?

I glance up.

Someone who looks every inch the successful businessman has stopped in front of me. He's short in stature and somewhat overweight. The fine cut of his suit tells me it's made to measure. His hair is greying at the temples, so I'd put him in his early fifties.

The pin badge on his lapel reveals he's a member of the local small-business association. I look down at the handmade shoes, which probably cost an average weekly wage. He places the large package he's carrying on the ground and smiles.

"Let's see what I can do for you."

I watch as he dips his hand into his trouser pocket and pulls out a silver clip containing a thick wad of notes.

From his gruff accent, you wouldn't know he's got money. My jaw drops as he peels off a twenty-pound note and bends to hand it to me.

I stretch forward and reach out gratefully.

But before my fingers are quite close enough, he snatches it back. Then I watch in horror as he produces a lighter from his pocket and sets fire to it.

"There we go. You wanted change. I've changed the cash into ashes." With that, he bursts out laughing, picks up his package and walks away.

I guess he must think I'm a dirty smelly homeless tramp, too lazy or drunk to find a job.

I get it. It happens a lot.

You've probably seen homeless people on the TV news, and you think it looks shocking. But have you ever wondered what it's really like? I mean, *really* like?

Unless you experience it for yourself, you'll never have an inkling of the cold that penetrates all the way down to your bones.

You'll never need to flinch at the sight of every moving shadow.

Or sleep with one eye open to check if the bunch of thugs who beat you up the other night are coming back to finish the job.

CHAPTER THIRTY-FIVE

JAMES

Tuesday 18th October 2016

Across the road from the grubby doorway where I'm sitting is a jewellery shop called Hurst & Co. Above the shop sign is a large brass clock with Roman numerals, telling me the time is five minutes to six. It's been about half an hour since the guy burned the twenty-pound note right before my eyes.

I'm about to leave when a young man walks past. He's someone I recognise. Two or three times a week, he'll drop me a fifty-pence or pound coin. On a few occasions, he's even handed me a sandwich and a hot coffee. I would guess he's in his late twenties.

He's looking a bit distracted, but suddenly, he stops, turns round, steps back, and drops a two-pound coin into my hat.

"There you go, mate. Tell you what... Buy yourself a Lotto ticket. It's a jackpot tonight – you might get lucky." As he walks away, he turns and gives me a smile and a thumbs-up for good luck.

Maybe he spent time on the streets when he was younger. Or he's simply a caring person. Whatever the reason, I'm grateful.

Soon after 'Lotto Boy', a young girl drops twenty pence and, with a soft voice, says: "I'm sorry, it's all I can spare."

Thank you, whoever you are. I'll take whatever I can, and I'm grateful to you for speaking to me like a human being.

It means, with the eighty pence of donations from the past three hours, I now have a total of three pounds.

Some days, this spot can be good, and I end up with between five and ten pounds. But today, even before the weather took a turn for the worse, no one seemed to notice me, or at least they pretended not to. If you don't want to give me money, I'd settle for a smile.

The clock above Hurst & Co has chimed six times, and this doorway doesn't provide much protection. When the wind picks up, the rain comes down at an angle, and it's difficult to shelter. So I decide now might be a good time to find a new spot.

I walk slower nowadays. My shoes are developing holes, my socks rub my feet, and besides, I'm not exactly in a hurry to get anywhere. I think I'll try my luck by the cash machine on the Market Square. I once got five pounds from an elderly couple who took pity on me. That's the most I've ever been given in one go.

Taking this route leads me along Market Street. Most of the shops are closed at this time of night, apart from Tindall's Convenience Store, which stays open until eleven.

As I walk past the door, I catch sight of the Lotto sign. I stop and think for a moment. What did he say? "*There you go, mate... Buy yourself a Lotto ticket – you might get lucky.*"

A voice inside me says: *What have you got to lose?* It's a

stupid question, as two pounds is two-thirds of my income for the day and would go a long way towards buying me a meal.

I'm surprised to find myself stepping inside. Nowadays, crowds are something I try to avoid, and this place is heaving.

The next thing I know, I'm filling in some random numbers at the Lotto stand, then I'm in the queue to buy my ticket. All three checkouts have a long line of people. Everyone is buying food, drink, and Lotto tickets.

There's a sign saying it's a record-breaking jackpot. I guess everyone's hoping they will win.

To pass the time while I wait in line, I look around at the other people in the queues. Observing people is one of the skills you learn as a detective. I watch the overweight girl buying magazines with diet plans on the cover. At the same time, she's holding a packet of chocolate digestives in her other hand. The middle-aged man is trying to hide a soft-porn magazine, covering it with a newspaper until it comes time to pay. I assume he's joined the longest queue because there's a man at the till.

I see a younger man, a shop worker by the look of his cheap suit, white shirt, and plain blue tie; he's hiding a computer magazine inside his jacket as he pays for another, creating his own illegal buy-one-get-one-free deal.

In the queue next to me, I notice the man who made out he was going to give me a twenty-pound note before he burned it. He has a Lotto form in his hand so, like me, he's buying a ticket. I hope *he* doesn't win.

In the other hand he's still carrying the large parcel he had when he burned the note, and has a roll of wrapping paper under his left arm. He's oblivious to everything and everyone around him.

He's raising his voice as he speaks on his mobile: "Listen,

you piece of crap. Get your act together and make sure my girls arrive on time for their appointments. Otherwise I'll come and break your legs. Do I make myself clear?"

Once I reach the counter, I hand over my money. In return, the machine dispenses a ticket. The shop assistant hands it to me, along with my receipt.

I make my way out of the store at the same time as 'Mr Loud'.

I see him turn his head to ogle an attractive young lady walking into the store. I look away from him for a moment as I take the last step from inside the doorway. It seems his actions have made him lose his balance, as he drops what he's carrying to reach out and grab the nearest thing to save himself from falling.

The only problem is that *thing* is me – he's a heavy man – and he takes me down with him, so we both end up sprawled across the exit.

My Lotto ticket falls to the floor between us, as does his parcel, the wrapping paper and even his mobile phone.

He quickly changes from being 'Mr Loud' into 'Mr Angry', and it appears what just happened is *my* fault.

He grabs me but soon lets go as he smells my, shall we say, lack of eau de toilette. He swears and curses, kicking out with his right foot. He screams, "Get away from me or I'll kill you, you human piece of crap."

I shudder, as from the tone of his voice, there could be some truth in his threat.

People make a wide detour around us. No one comes to help. I can't say I blame them. He makes a menacing figure in his rage, and besides, it's all over in a few seconds.

I scramble across the shop floor and reach out for my Lotto ticket. I manage to retrieve it after he lands his second kick. I use the upright post of the shop's exit door to get to my feet and scuttle out as quickly as I can. The words that reverberate around my head are the last thing I heard him say. He called me a "human piece of crap".

It was a mistake to have gone into the shop. I need to gain as much distance as I can from this guy.

As I make my retreat, I can see him on his hands and knees, scrabbling around to find his belongings, still swearing and cursing.

My experience over the past few months has taught me to keep out of trouble, even if it means backing down. In better times, as a former police detective, I would have stood my ground, but things have changed.

Nowadays I don't walk down the pavement like normal people do. I scurry along like a rat, keeping to the inside, following the contour of every building. I've changed from a person into a shadow figure. I no longer look people in the eye. As I walk the streets, I tend to look down, so I can tell you a lot about people's footwear!

I've learned where every alleyway is, where it leads, and which shop doorways or recesses will offer me cover. Doorways to churches, meeting rooms and building exits have become my natural haunts. I see things hidden from other people. It's the best way to survive.

After what I've just been through, I'm shaking a little – more than a little, if I'm being honest. I put it down to the rain and the cold of the night. I'm not normally frightened by such things. But, deep down, I know it's the tone of Mr Angry's voice that's making me quiver.

But the most frightening thing is – I have a really bad feeling our paths will cross again.

CHAPTER THIRTY-SIX

DAVE

Tuesday evening, 18th October 2016

For Dave Rex, it's been a nightmare of a day. To start with, the lady who cleans his house twice a week called in sick, and he hates the place not being spotless. It also meant she wasn't there to take in the parcel he was expecting, so he had to wait for the delivery man.

Dave owns a laptop, but he's never bothered to learn about computers. He's worried things can be traced too easily. He certainly doesn't want to record all his shady business dealings on one, and after going online to order a gift for his mother's birthday last week, he's in no hurry to repeat the experience. He thought it would be straightforward.

He wanted to buy something special for her. The website he visited offered to gift-wrap the item – the main reason he ordered it from them in the first place.

Dave's planning to spend a few hours with her today before leaving for a fortnight's holiday at his villa. But when his package fails to arrive by mid-afternoon, he tries to contact the company.

As he searches their website, he murmurs, "For fuck's sake. Why don't they put a phone number where you can easily find it?"

It takes him an hour to find the number. And when he finally manages to get through to someone, he's informed that he'd filled out the wrong date. The customer service person apologises but tells him it isn't due to be delivered until *next* Tuesday.

Today, of all days, this was not what he needed.

Finally, he had to drive into Trentbridge town centre and spend time walking around the shops. It took him over two hours to find an alternative gift. Unfortunately, the store didn't offer a gift-wrapping service. So, he had to visit a convenience store, buy wrapping paper, take it home and waste more time wrapping it.

He loves his old mum. It's not her fault he's in a rage. The day's unplanned events meant he only managed to spend half an hour with her. When he gets back, he's promised to take her for a nice meal at her favourite restaurant.

He's had to rush to deliver her present. Then ignore the speed limit to get to the airport in time to catch his late-night flight to Murcia Airport in Spain.

Sitting with a glass of wine by his side, Dave sighs with relief. Despite everything, he arrived at the airport just in time to catch his flight.

As the jet soars above the clouds and into the night sky, all his cares and worries seem to melt away.

Dave kicks off his shoes. He thinks back to the incident with the tramp who got in his way and tripped him up. Dave only went into the convenience store to buy wrapping paper and a Lotto ticket. What happened on his way out didn't help his high blood pressure.

Cursing and swearing as he stomped away from Tindall's, he'd tried his best to brush the dirt off his smart trousers. But even now, he's sure he can still smell the stench of that filthy tramp.

Dave's thoughts are interrupted by the voice of the flight attendant. After rushing around all day, he hasn't had time to eat anything. So he's happy to see her standing there with his order of spicy green Thai curry.

"Here you are, sir. Be careful. The plate is hot. Can I get you another glass of wine?"

"Yes, that would be most welcome."

Thinking about his meal, Dave is reminded of his kebab shop. To help get more customers, he had people put large posters all the way along Woolston Road. A rival takeaway owner made the mistake of threatening to tear them down.

So the first thing Dave did was smash his rival's shop windows after they had closed for the night.

When this failed to stop the owner of Tasty Kebabs complaining, Dave visited his shop in the early hours of the morning. He ran a hose through the letterbox, poured petrol in and set light to it. Luckily, a passer-by noticed the fire and dialled 999.

The local paper covered the story. They reported the fire brigade chief saying: "It was a miracle that none of the people in the upstairs flat were killed or seriously injured. Five minutes later, there would have been fatalities."

That same night, the shop owner received a note in his letterbox. 'Keep quiet, or your house will be next.' He was too frightened to go to the police.

A similar thing happened when Dave bought his second business, Trent Taxis. He got his control room to listen in on the radio calls of his main rivals, Cresta Cabs, then sent his taxis to arrive before theirs and steal their fares.

When they discovered what was happening, the two brothers who ran Cresta came to see him. Dave and three of his accomplices beat them up. They put them in the boot of an old taxi. Then they dumped them, battered and bruised, on the pavement outside their own taxi office.

The next day, Dave phoned them and made an offer to buy their business for half its true value. When they refused, they started getting messages from an untraceable pay-as-you-go mobile. It showed photos of their wives and children, saying things like: 'Whoops. Almost ran over your daughter as she left school today.'

After two weeks of constant messages and late-night silent phone calls, the two brothers decided to accept Dave's offer.

As he sips his wine, he allows himself a smile at his latest business purchase. The irony of using a launderette to help launder the cash isn't lost on him.

As he finishes his wine, the pilot announces, "Ladies and gentlemen. Please fasten your seat belts. We are about to start our descent."

Dave is looking forward to arriving at his beautiful villa. Once he's had a good night's rest and spent some time soaking up the sun, he will set about thinking up new ways to ensure that the tax authorities and police believe the top-of-the-range Mercedes, the luxury foreign villa and the expensive lifestyle are funded entirely from his honest endeavours.

CHAPTER THIRTY-SEVEN

JAMES

Wednesday 19th October 2016

I'm still shaking a little from yesterday's confrontation with Mr Angry. I can't seem to get it out of my thoughts. It still sends a shiver down my spine. So much so that I've hardly slept.

Perhaps my weekly visit to St Matthew's Church Hall will help get it out of my mind. I certainly hope so.

I come here every Wednesday. It's run by a lady called Emily and a small team of volunteers. They offer a lovely cup of tea and a range of delicious homemade cakes to anyone who is homeless or in need.

It opens at ten, and it looks like I'm the first 'customer' to arrive today. I walk up to the counter.

"Hello, dear. Cup of tea with three sugars and a slice of fruit cake, as usual, is it?"

"Yes please, that would be lovely."

"Still got the sweet tooth then?"

"Yes, when the cake is as delicious as yours."

"That's very kind of you. There you go. Enjoy."

"Thank you, Emily."

"My pleasure, dear. It's nice to serve someone with manners."

On rainy days like today, after my free food and a cuppa, I usually head for the local library. Not the main town centre library. I prefer the one on Lockwood Road. I stroll along Fenton Road and turn to walk the twenty yards up Lockwood.

The entrance consists of a huge grey stone surround, which must be twenty feet high. It dwarfs a double doorway, and on either side of it are three rows of windows.

The library is small but friendly and warm. Before mid-afternoon, there are usually only a handful of people, most of them there to return books and choose new ones.

As you walk in through the automatic doors, the entire area in front of you is filled with endless volumes. The counter is to the right, and further along is an enclosed space for the children's section.

I always turn left and head for the reference section. This is where anyone can sit and read a variety of daily newspapers and a wide selection of magazines.

I started coming to this library when I was growing up, and it's where I used to bring my kids. That's why I like to come here. It evokes fond memories.

The head librarian is an old-school type. Miss Hartman has time for everyone. She's been here so long she must be close to retirement, but she never married. I heard that her fiancé died while saving someone from drowning, two weeks before their wedding day.

She's a petite lady and reminds me of my old history teacher. I guess it's the thick-rimmed glasses that seem to be too heavy for her nose, and her short neat stylish brown hair. She's extremely knowledgeable on most subjects. And like a walking encyclopaedia on local history.

Miss Hartman is aware I was a police officer. She knows what happened to my family and my current situation.

Without an address, I'm not eligible for a library card. So she keeps the books I'm reading behind the counter until my next visit. My current book is *Too Close for Comfort* by Adam Croft. I'm about a third of the way through and can't wait to finish it to find out what happens.

I walk over to the rack of newspapers. I study the headlines for something to grab my attention.

I settle on the *Daily Mail*. I'll save reading my novel for later.

As I walk over to my favourite seat by the window, I glance over to Miss Hartman and wave politely. She returns it with a lovely and genuine smile.

Looking around, before I start to read, I notice there are only three other people in the library. Two are busy choosing new books. The third is a few feet away, using the photocopier located next to the row of computers. I turn back to the newspaper and read.

The front page of the *Mail* carries the usual type of story – ongoing rows between the two main political parties.

Inside is a range of stories detailing the misery going on around the world, punctuated by opinion columns, each more ready than the last to force their own viewpoint onto anyone prepared to read their rants.

The level of interest I can muster means it only takes me

about twenty minutes or so to reach the back cover. I'm not interested in reading the adverts for the sea cruise holidays. If I were, the time to read it would almost certainly double.

Next, I decide to read the *Sun*. I often do the Sudoku puzzle, as it's a way of passing some time.

I'm about to return the paper to the rack when I remember the Lotto ticket in the back pocket of my trousers. I placed it in this pocket because I'm certain it doesn't have any holes and, furthermore, it's secured by a button.

On the rare occasion I have something important to keep, this is the pocket I use. The others all have holes.

Turning to the newspaper's results, I place the ticket down on the table and check it against the numbers. Much to my disappointment, only one of the numbers matches. My finger is still on the ticket when I notice Miss Hartman standing over me, clutching my current book. She glances down.

"You're checking the wrong ones. Those are the National Lottery numbers. The ticket you're holding is for the Euro."

"I didn't realise there were two different ones," I answer. "It's just that someone said it could be my lucky day, so I thought it was worth a go."

"*Someone* has to win," she replies with a smile. "You could be Mr Lucky today."

The thought comes into my head. *Yeah, some chance of that.*

I watch as Miss Hartman returns to the enquiries counter to deal with a lady waiting to check out some books.

I'm not holding out much hope with the Lotto. The *Sun* newspaper I was reading a few minutes ago said this was the largest jackpot ever. The article said the likelihood of someone winning is one chance in a hundred and thirty-nine million. Apparently there's more prospect of being struck by lightning – twice!

The money I wasted on the ticket could have paid for a burger from McDonald's. What was I thinking?

Checking it would be a complete waste of time.

I screw up the ticket and throw it in the rubbish bin.

CHAPTER THIRTY-EIGHT

DAVE

Wednesday 19th October 2016

The taxi ride from the airport to Dave's villa in La Manga has taken a little over an hour. The skill of the driver has made it a smooth ride. Dave is grateful for the fact the man kept his mouth shut for the entire journey.

Dave presses a button on his key fob and the electronic gates open to allow the taxi to pull up to the front of the villa.

The driver takes the two suitcases from the boot and places them down close to the stairs in the spacious hallway.

In return, he walks out with his fare plus a generous tip.

Dave strolls to the kitchen. He checks that the housekeeper has filled the fridge and drinks cabinet, as he requested. Yes, it all looks good.

Taking his suitcases upstairs, he is delighted to see crisp fresh bed sheets. He slips in between them and within five minutes is peacefully snoring.

The next morning, the alarm clock on his bedside table wakes Dave at nine a.m. He jumps in the shower, then chooses a set of casual clothes from his walk-in closet. He makes his way downstairs to find the housekeeper in the kitchen. She serves up his breakfast and places a cut-glass jug of freshly squeezed orange juice on the table.

"Good morning, Mr Rex. It's lovely to have you back."

"Good morning, Isabella. It's nice to be back. How are all your family?"

"Yes, they are good. Thank you for asking."

Dave purchased the Spanish-style villa four years ago.

He'd been staying at a nearby rental villa and noticed the 'For Sale' sign. The owner was happy to do a deal where part of the price was declared, and part was paid in untraceable cash.

The villa boasts a swimming pool, a front terrace, five bedrooms, and a patio. It also has a large expensively fitted-out kitchen-diner. Every room has air-conditioning. The garden is gorgeous and of a good size, with tall trees that offer complete privacy on all sides. There is also a large rooftop sun terrace with great views of the nearby area.

The villa is larger than he needs. However, the location provides a higher degree of privacy than the other properties he viewed, having no close neighbours and being located at the end of a quiet road, with private access to a clean sandy beach. There are shops a few hundred metres away, and on Sundays, a busy market.

The area abounds with good restaurants and cafés. But for Dave, the main attraction is the fact that the area is a golfers' paradise. It has no fewer than sixteen golf clubs.

These include six Jack Nicklaus courses. There are also

three championship courses at the world-renowned Manga Club, all within a thirty-minute drive.

After an enjoyable day of golf followed by a delicious meal in the clubhouse, Dave returns to his villa.

The temperature has dropped to a pleasant twenty-four degrees. Dave sits at a large table on the patio and lays out the file of notes and ideas he has compiled over recent weeks.

His plans for the future are simple, the way he likes things.

He has always been good at planning and scheming.

Yes, he will enjoy two weeks in the sun. And the man who, yesterday, helped to put him in such a foul mood, the one he called a 'human piece of crap', is, for all he knows, lying in a gutter somewhere. In fact, Dave hopes he is. It would serve him right!

CHAPTER THIRTY-NINE

JAMES

Wednesday 19th October 2016

I wander over to the unisex toilet, say goodbye to Emily's cup of tea, and wash my hands.

Maybe I'll go over to the seat near the large window and pick up where I left off with the Adam Croft novel I've been reading.

After a minute, I change my mind.

I know it'll be a complete waste of time but I have nothing better to do, so checking the numbers will kill a couple of minutes. If I match two numbers, it should be enough to buy a meal.

I retrieve the Lotto ticket from the bin and flatten out the creases. I lay the newspaper down and make sure I'm checking it against the correct game this time.

I start to check the numbers.

Hey, two numbers match.

Three numbers, then four, five, six, seven.

They all match.

I carefully check them again.

One by one, they match the numbers on my still slightly crumpled ticket.

I triple-check the numbers; then check them a fourth time. It's the same result. They all match.

My hands are shaking. I stand and accidentally bump against a bookcase, knocking several books to the floor.

Within a few seconds, Miss Hartman appears. "Are you unwell?"

"Eh, eh," is all I can utter. "Can you check these numbers for me?" I whisper, so as not to attract attention from the girl using the photocopier. Fortunately, her back is turned, and the copier is humming away.

Miss Hartman runs her finger along the line of numbers on my ticket as she carefully checks them off. I watch as she looks at the date on my ticket to make sure it's the same one printed in the newspaper.

After what seems like an hour, she responds in a soft voice, "According to the evidence, you have won the Lotto. Congratulations."

"What do I do?"

"You contact the Lotto company to stake your claim. But, before you do, you need to put your details on the back to prove it's your ticket." She takes a breath. "I'll get you a pen."

When she returns, I follow her instructions. I put my name and signature onto the back of the ticket where it says, 'Sign Your Ticket, Make It Yours'.

Miss Hartman continues. "I've just been on their website. The best thing you can do is phone and tell them you have a winning ticket."

"But I don't have access to a phone."

"Under the circumstances, I think it would be all right

for you to use the phone in the staff room. Here's the number you need to dial." With that, she hands me a piece of paper with a telephone number neatly written down.

She leads me across the library to a door with a frosted-glass-panelled top section. She keys a set of numbers into the security pad.

It's a large room with a tiny kitchen area on the right-hand side. On the left is a small office with a beech desk and a large corkboard on the wall above it. Miss Hartman points to the blue telephone on the desk.

"Dial nine for an outside line then the number I've given you," she tells me. "And good luck!" She walks out, closing the door softly behind her.

My first thought is to go back and check all the numbers again, but I know I've already done this. Once more won't change things.

I sit at the desk. My stomach flutters and the palms of my hands are covered in sweat. What if I've got it all wrong? It would be embarrassing to come back to the library, and it's the best place to spend the long hours of the day.

I sit here going back and forth. *Should I or shouldn't I?*

Finally, I pick up the phone, remember to dial nine, and, one by one, slowly press each number listed on the sheet of paper.

A female voice answers after three rings.

"Hello. I'm, umm, er, not sure. I've checked the numbers several times, and they seem correct. I think I've, er, won the EuroMillions Jackpot."

"Congratulations! I just need to go over a few details with you." The lady on the phone is calm. She sounds like this happens on a regular basis.

I give her all the information she asks for.

"I just need to check a few extra things," she says. "Can you give me a phone number where I can contact you in about an hour?"

"Can you hang on a minute? I don't have my own phone."

I go and find Miss Hartman and explain the situation.

She jots down a phone number on a piece of paper and hands it to me. "Ask them to call you back on this number. You can wait here until they ring."

After Miss Hartman keys the numbers into the entry pad for access to the staff room, I go back to the desk and pick up the phone. "I've got a number where you can call me back." I give the lady the phone number, and, once the call has ended, I sit at the desk.

I put my head in my hands, as I'm not sure what's going on. I feel confused. Is this really happening?

Twenty minutes later, the phone rings. The woman, who identifies herself as Linda, tells me she needs to ask me some more questions. She starts by asking where and when I bought the ticket. I tell her, and add that I still have the shop receipt with the ticket, and she tells me that's really helpful.

She says she can see no problem at this stage, but cannot confirm my win. She explains it needs to be checked by the company coordinator.

She then tells me they'll be sending one of their counsellors to help and advise me about what happens next, and at this point, she asks for my address. I call in Miss Hartman to speak with Linda, and they work out a time to meet me at the library. She says I can meet them in the staff room, and no one will disturb us.

I'm a rational person, yet it's still hard to believe this is happening. *Have I really won the Lotto?* I'm not even sure why I bought a ticket in the first place. *What was I thinking?*

I need time to get my head around this. I tell myself not to get overexcited, just in case. But she told me. I know she did. I heard her say it; Linda from the Lotto company told me.

She said that I hold the only winning ticket and that it's the largest amount in the company's history. Linda told me I've won. I couldn't quite take it in, so I wrote the amount down: £168,548,030.

Surely this sort of thing doesn't happen to someone like me? I don't deserve to win! Oh, God. If only Miriam were here, and Jack and Abi. It's not fair. Really not fair.

Linda said the people from the company will be there to meet me tomorrow. *What people? What will they want me to do?* My head's spinning. I can feel one of my migraine headaches coming on. Believe it or not, winning a hundred and sixty-eight million pounds is extremely stressful.

Even when I had a family, I would play the Lotto only on odd occasions. Winning enough to pay off the mortgage was about as much as I could imagine. Like most people, I guess I was thinking, *If only.*

So, what the hell does a homeless man need with all that money? The truth is I didn't expect to win. I got carried away in the moment. Maybe I wanted enough to get off the streets and have a little bit left over. *But a hundred and sixty-eight million pounds! What the hell do I do with that? I could give most of it to charity. I hope the Lotto people will be able to advise me.*

After my phone conversation with Linda, I thank Miss Hartman and leave the library in a daze. It's only four o'clock. Do I tell anyone? Who can I tell? Stevie's back in Rhyl and I don't have his contact details.

The migraine is getting worse. I think I'll go back to the Albion and try to sleep. I know it won't be dark for a couple of hours and I'm not sure what I'll find there. I never go back until the evening, long after the top management have gone home. I don't want to get found out or cause any trouble.

Still, I'll make an exception today, as my head feels like someone's hitting it from the inside with a sledgehammer.

I may be a multi-millionaire, but at this precise moment, I can't even afford to buy a packet of Nurofen.

I'm meeting with the Lotto people in the morning, so this time tomorrow, I'll be rich beyond my wildest dreams.

With all that money, I'm set for life.

So why do I have the feeling something is about to go wrong?

CHAPTER FORTY

JAMES

Friday 21st October 2016

The *Trentbridge Times* newspaper carries the headline 'Local Homeless Man Wins £168 Million Lotto'. It includes a photo of me holding up a giant cheque. I'm surrounded by scantily clad women showering me with champagne.

The Lotto people have persuaded me to go public. It's done with the understanding the media won't be given details about the death of my family or my background as a police officer. Fortunately, they don't seem interested in any of this. All they want is the story of my life on the streets.

They take photos of my worn-out clothes and shoes stuffed with cardboard to cover holes. They love the quote I give them about wearing a new brand of deodorant; I tell them it's called 'Smellalot', and I add, "Last time I looked, it wasn't a brand you would find behind the men's counter at John Lewis or Boots." This goes down well.

The only thing they want is the rags-to-riches story and

some before-and-after photos. I take them to West Street and show them the vacant shop doorway.

Then we visit M&S, where they buy me a set of smart new clothes. Then it's back to the empty shop doorway where I stand holding up bundles of fake cash so they can have *after* photos.

This is not serious journalism. They don't bother to check their facts. They even get my name slightly wrong. Instead of James Sheldon, in the newspapers they say my name is Anthony Sheldon. Anthony's my middle name. I guess they never let the facts get in the way of a good story. And stories that are a little over the top sell more newspapers.

I think these people live in a different world to normal folk. For them, everything needs to be blown out of all proportion. They're only happy when you make it bigger and brighter. For example, you don't receive the giant cheque you see in the photos; it's just part of the big PR publicity campaign in front of the cameras, for the benefit of the newspapers and TV. The money is transferred into your bank account. My bank account's been closed since the house was repossessed.

One of the team from the Lotto company takes me to the local branch of Lloyds Bank. It appears they're more than happy to open a new account when they hear how much I'm paying in.

It's been a week, and the initial excitement of my win has died down. I'm no longer the main topic of conversation or making front-page news. People now have other things to talk about.

A visit to a local barbershop has removed my scraggy beard and given me an expensive new hairstyle. An eye test at the optician's has given me a pair of prescription glasses. I've also purchased new clothes.

Now I can walk down the street, and no one recognises me. The only people who hassle me are homeless people asking if I can spare any change. I hand each of them a twenty-pound note, without taking it back and burning it.

The Lotto people have given me a letter from their CEO. It congratulates me on becoming their biggest-ever prize winner. It states I hold the only winning ticket for their prize draw of one hundred and sixty-eight million, five hundred and forty-eight thousand, and thirty pounds. I carry the letter with me, unfold it, and read it about six times a day. I still have to pinch myself to confirm this is real.

The main thing that keeps going around in my head is that nobody needs this much money. My thinking is that if I give away one hundred and fifty million, it will leave me with eighteen million. That will allow me to spend eight million on... well, anything I want and still have ten million. If I live for the next forty years, that works out to five thousand pounds a week, ten times the average weekly wage. How would you need to spend more than that?

And a hundred and fifty million could help a lot of people, but how?

That's the part I'm still working on.

CHAPTER FORTY-ONE

JAMES

Friday 21st October 2016

Rather than stay at the Albion Hotel, I've decided to book into the Premier Inn. No one here knows me, so I can be left alone to think about what the future holds.

I can afford to eat in the best places, but I prefer plain food. The hotel restaurant is fine. I order a hamburger and chips and a glass of lemonade.

While I wait for it to arrive, I take out a notebook I purchased during an earlier visit to Ryman's. I'm trying to come up with ideas to give away a hundred and fifty million pounds. It's not as easy as you might imagine.

After enjoying the main course, I glance at the desserts. They all look tempting, but my stomach is not accustomed to eating a large meal. I decide I'll pass, this time.

As the waitress comes to take away my empty plate, I ask her what made her decide on a career in hotels. She tells me it's a stopgap before she goes to university.

"I'm planning to study Business Management and

Human Resources at Nottingham Trent Uni. One of my teachers told me it would be a good career," she tells me.

As she wanders off to serve another guest, my thoughts turn to my own school days.

When I was eight, we moved to Trentbridge. I recall Mum telling me it was because Dad got a promotion.

So we would be moving here because he had been put in charge of running a factory.

We moved into a nice house with a lovely garden. Our next-door neighbours were a policeman and his family. I became best friends with their son, Oliver. He would tell me stories about his dad's life in the police force. I guess that's where my interest began.

Every week, I would save my pocket money to buy books on real-life crime detection, crime scene investigations (CSI) and forensics.

I remember when my dad was on the early shift. He'd meet me after school, and we would go to the park. He would push me on the swings and play with my friends and me.

He'd buy us all an ice cream and set up goalposts for football. He'd be the referee and he was always fair. My dad was such a lovely man. He was my hero.

One day, when I expected to see him outside school, he wasn't there. I walked home on my own. I found him sitting on the sofa. It looked like he'd been crying. I'd never seen him do that before. He told me he'd been made redundant. I wasn't sure what that meant. I was only ten.

According to what Mum told me, the factory had been taken over by a large American company. Initially, they promised to keep it open, but then they went back on their word and closed it down.

Mum said that Dad tried to find a new job, but times

were hard. One day I came home from school to find a removal lorry outside. We moved to a first-floor flat on a not-very-nice council estate.

Looking back, I can see that losing our lovely home affected Dad more than he let on. I guess he felt he was a failure now that he couldn't provide for his family. He started drinking and getting violent.

One day, he got so drunk he fell down a flight of stairs. The hospital did all it could, but it wasn't enough. Dad was dead.

So it was just Mum and me. A week after that, I started a new school, but I had to walk past our old house every day. That was hard.

Money was tight, and Mum couldn't afford to give me pocket money. Somehow, she managed to save up and buy me a bike for my eleventh birthday. I'd only had it for two weeks before it was stolen, so I had to give up my paper round.

That was when I learned about the local library. All the books I couldn't afford to buy, I could borrow. It was a revelation.

Mum always encouraged me. She said that if I did well in my exams and got good grades, I'd always be able to find a job. She said Dad had often talked about improving his education but never got around to it.

I guess it all helped to spur me on, and I won a place at Manchester University.

That's where I met Miriam. I knew instantly that we were meant for each other.

I'd known what I wanted to do from the age of ten. I joined the police service direct from university.

By the time I was twenty-six, I'd made it to detective sergeant. I loved every minute of it. One week, I'd be dealing with murder or gang-related crime, the next, it could be cybercrime or something drugs-related. I was proud to be part of a team that took a lot of nasty people off the streets.

However it's nothing like you see on TV shows. One investigation can take months of painstaking work. Especially where gangs are concerned. They threaten the families of anyone likely to 'grass' on them. For the most part, the people I worked with were all good coppers.

There were a couple I suspected of being corrupt, but I had no proof and tried to avoid them whenever possible. It doesn't pay to make enemies, so I was pleasant but never went for a drink with them. Luckily they didn't ask me to, and, likewise, I didn't ask them.

During your daily duties as a senior detective, you never know who you're going to meet. So, you always have to look the part. My choice was to wear a nice suit, a silk tie, good quality shoes, and Tom Ford Sole di Positano fragrance for men. And I tried to always have fresh breath.

When my family was killed, I was about to be promoted to detective inspector. It would have meant I'd oversee a lot of major investigations.

Things are very different now. That life is behind me.

I'm brought back to the present by someone at the next table scraping their chair. I look up and notice the restaurant is getting crowded.

I head up to my room, sit at the desk at the end of the king-size Hypnos bed, and continue finishing off my masterplan.

I think about the hundred and sixty-eight million and

allow myself one last self-doubt that this is a dream. I decide it isn't, and enough is enough. God has chosen me to do something good with this money, and I'm not about to let him down.

CHAPTER FORTY-TWO

JAMES

Wednesday 26th October 2016

I have a busy day planned, so I head down to breakfast at seven thirty.

The Lotto organisation people have been really good when it comes to providing me with help and advice.

They've arranged a string of appointments. I'm meeting with financial advisers to ensure I don't go on a massive spending spree. They'll give me advice to keep my new-found fortune safe, and prevent me blowing my brains out over the kind of excess brought about by this scale of sudden wealth.

At the meetings, it's agreed I'll have two savings accounts: one with Lloyds and one with Coutts & Co., bankers for the monarchy. If it's good enough for royalty, it's good enough for me. I've always respected the royal family.

The financial advisers suggest I leave five million in each account. The rest will be placed into short-term investment plans, which will pay interest.

By the time all the meetings and appointments set for today are concluded, the time is five-twenty p.m.

Twenty-five minutes later, I'm standing on West Street. This time, I'm not sitting in a shop doorway begging for spare change with a hat.

There's someone I used to see walk past at around this time of day. I'm anxious to speak with them, so I stand in the doorway I know so well. The big difference today is that, rather than being in my old threadbare clothes, I'm smartly dressed. My new shoes are shiny, comfortable and, most importantly, won't let in water like my old ones did.

I watch all the people rushing home from work.

Suddenly, I see a young girl I recognise and step forward.

"Excuse me, miss. I'm sorry to bother you. In the past, I've seen you walking along here with a young man who usually wears grey trousers and a tan jacket."

She stops. In my previous state, she probably would have rushed away, but now I look respectable, and the smile on my face helps. It should do – one of the appointments I had today was for an orthodontist. I couldn't believe how much it cost to go private rather than on the NHS. Three hundred pounds for a one-hour session. Still, at least my teeth look healthy again.

It takes the young lady a couple of seconds to think.

"Oh, you mean Martin. I'm sorry, but I don't work with him anymore. He was made redundant last week."

"Can you tell me how to get hold of him please? It's rather important."

"You could ask my branch manager. He'll have his address. All I know is, he lives on Primrose Square, but I don't know the number. The manager will be in tomorrow. It's the Norwood Building Society on High Street."

I could wait until tomorrow and speak with Martin's manager. But I decide not to. I don't have anything better to do, so I walk around the corner into Townsend Place, which is the town's central bus station, and over to the taxi rank.

"Primrose Square please."

The journey takes a little over ten minutes.

"Which number?" enquires the driver.

"Drop me on the corner here." I pay the fare with a twenty-pound note and let him keep the change. "Here goes nothing," I say to myself as I walk up the path to the first house, number 12.

I knock at the door. "Hello. I'm sorry to bother you, but I'm looking for the house of a young man called Martin. He worked at the Norwood Building Society. Can you help me?"

"No, never 'eard of 'im," comes the reply, and the door is slammed in my face.

I've done this sort of thing before in my days as a detective.

You don't knock at every door. I walk along for ten houses and knock at number 32. All the even numbers are on the same side of the road.

This time a lady answers, "I'm not sure, but I have a feeling he lives at number 48. You could try there."

I thank her and walk down a further eight houses until I reach what I hope is the right house and ring the bell. A young lady comes to the door.

"Hello. I hope I've got the right house. I'm looking for Martin, who works, sorry, worked, at the Norwood Building Society on the High Street. A lady down the street told me he lives here."

"I'm Martin's wife," she replies. "He's popped down to

the shop, but he should be back in a couple of minutes. Is there anything I can help you with?"

"He gave me some money, and I'd like to pay him back."

Before she can answer, I hear footsteps behind me, and the young man I now know as Martin appears.

"Martin," his wife calls out, "this man says you lent him some money and he wants to pay it back."

"I'm sorry, sir, any money you may have borrowed from the building society should be repaid to them. Unfortunately I don't work there anymore. I can give you the name of the person to contact if you'd like."

I smile. "This has nothing to do with the building society. You may not be aware, but you gave me some money personally, and I've come to repay you, with interest. Can I take a minute of your time please?"

Martin raises his eyebrows and shrugs. "I guess that will be all right, but I'm not sure how I can help. You'd better come in. We'll talk about it over a cup of tea."

We go into a small but very well-presented front room. It's obvious that, although it hasn't cost a lot to decorate and furnish, they have taste, and care about their home.

"Please, sit down." Martin gestures to a single chair next to the sofa.

"You don't recognise me, do you?" I ask as he takes a seat at the end of the sofa closest to me.

"No, I'm very sorry. I'm usually good with faces, but I don't recognise you." As he speaks, he leans forward. "Could you please explain what this is all about?"

Martin's wife brings the tea through with a plate of assorted biscuits and sits down beside her husband.

I explain. "For the past ten months, I've been sitting in a doorway on West Street, cold, hungry, and homeless. On several occasions when you passed by, you were kind enough to bring me sandwiches and hot coffee. Rarely did a day go by when you didn't put fifty pence or a pound into my hat. A couple of weeks ago, you gave me two pounds and suggested I spend it on a Lotto ticket because it could be my lucky day."

"Yes, I vaguely remember," replies Martin.

"I did what you suggested, and my numbers came up – I won the Lotto. So I've come to pay back the two pounds plus a little interest on the money and to thank you for your kindness. Can I ask what your surname is?"

"It's Hammond."

I take the cheque from my jacket pocket and fill in his name above the amount I've already written out. I hand it to him.

He looks at me, looks at the cheque, then back at me.

After a pause of a few seconds, his mouth drops open. "There must be some mistake."

"No mistake," I reply. "Haven't you seen the news of the homeless man who won the Lotto? That was me. Without you, I wouldn't have won a penny, so I figure it's only fair."

Still looking at me, Martin passes the cheque across to his wife, whose eyes flicker between Martin and the cheque.

"It says two million pounds," she says.

"That's correct. Two pounds paid back with interest – and gratitude."

"Is this for real?" asks Martin.

"I wouldn't kid you. I guarantee this is genuine, and you can pay it in tomorrow. I'll phone the bank in the morning and tell them to expect it."

"I don't know what to say, except thank you, thank you so much," says Martin as his wife begins to cry.

"You don't know what this means to us," she says.

"Oh, I think I do," I reply, "and I want you to enjoy every single penny of it. Don't go wild. Invest it wisely for your family."

They hug me, and I leave with a tear in my eye and a warm feeling in my heart. If this is how good it feels to give money away, I'm going to be doing a lot more of it.

I'll start tomorrow.

There are two other people I'd like to thank.

CHAPTER FORTY-THREE

JAMES

For a man of the cloth in his mid-fifties, Wendall Bates, vicar of St Matthew's Church, is very switched on about the digital world. He's read about people contacting you pretending to be police officers or purporting to be from the bank to get your account details before emptying your account, and, therefore, the phone call I made earlier, asking to make a donation into the church bank account, aroused suspicion.

However, I told him I understood his concerns and suggested it might be better if I were to visit the church and make the donation directly.

This is why, three hours later, as I enter, I see Wendall standing next to the altar.

"Hello, I'm James Sheldon. We spoke on the phone earlier."

"Hello. Wendall Bates. It's nice to meet you." He gives me a big genuine grin.

"Wendall, I'll come straight to the point. I've witnessed

first-hand the wonderful things you do at the church hall and on Festival Place with the mobile tea stall, and I'd like to show my appreciation for what you did when I was in, shall we say, a less fortunate position." I put my hand inside my right-hand jacket pocket and pull out a cheque. "I wasn't sure who to make it out to..."

"Please make it out to St Matthew's Church Fund. That would be fine."

I sit on one of the pews, take my Parker pen from my inside jacket pocket and add the name to the amount I've already filled in. "I hope this helps with your appeal," I say as I hand the cheque over.

"We currently need to raise £30,000 for the church roof and any donation helps us enormously," explains Wendall.

He lifts his glasses, hanging from a cord across his chest, and looks at the cheque. "I don't mean to be rude or ungrateful, but is this some sort of prank? This cheque's for £30,000, the entire amount."

I give a little laugh. "No, it's genuine. Before I won the Lotto, I was living on the streets and depended on handouts. When I needed food and drink, the kind people of this church were on hand to help. This is my way of saying thank you. I ask one favour: please keep my donation private. No publicity or details of where it came from."

"You have my word. This is such a relief. Now we can get the work underway. It's been a big worry for the past few months. God bless you."

"I think he already has, and now it's my turn to help others. Thank you for everything your church, and the people associated with it, are doing for the homeless. I can assure you; it really means a lot. I know you get little thanks, but, deep inside, I'm sure every single person you help is truly grateful – although many might not say it. Will you thank all your volunteers for me?"

Wendall promises he will, and, as I leave, I see him kneel down to offer a prayer.

I'm just thankful that I could answer one of them.

CHAPTER FORTY-FOUR

JAMES

Thursday 27th October 2016

Today is special in many ways. It's the first time I've ever walked through the front entrance of the Albion Hotel. I'm here to say a massive thank you to two wonderful people.

George Leeman, the night porter, doesn't start work until eight p.m., but I know he hangs around the hotel from about lunchtime. He once told me why. The tiny bedsit where he lives has problems with unemployed neighbours. They don't get up until early afternoon, then they spend the rest of the day blaring out music while he's trying to rest. So, he grabs what sleep he can then comes to the hotel for some peace and quiet.

The Albion has been a fixture in Trentbridge for as long as most people can remember. Located on Shaw Street, it sits on a prime site in the centre of town and even has its own car park. It was once the smartest meeting point in town, and it's still a popular place for people to stay.

The outside façade still reeks of pre-war high society.

You can tell it must have been magnificent once. Sadly, time has taken its toll, and the exterior is showing its age a little.

Seven days a week, one of the duty managers will arrive just before six a.m. They take over from the night porter and let in the kitchen staff, who begin work at six thirty.

Most of them enter via the main entrance. There are four people who usually come in through the kitchen rear entrance, as it's closer to their bus stop. I know only two of them by name.

Stella Young is a waitress in the restaurant and bar. I would guess she's in her late thirties or early forties. Some people find her a little snooty. I'm told there was once a Mr Young. The word is he found her entertaining another man in their bedroom, walked out, and never returned.

The other person is Freddie Brown. He's a young lad, around nineteen or twenty. Whatever he lacks in experience, he makes up for with elbow grease. He's always eager to help and is a hard worker. He's been working here for about a year, and everyone seems to like him.

When you first get to know him, he seems shy, but he seems to enjoy chatting with people. When I lived at the rear of the hotel, he was always friendly. He spoke to me in the same way he would talk to his best mate, despite the age difference. That meant a lot to me.

His main shortcoming is that he's a heavy smoker and stinks of cigarettes. However, his clothes are always clean, and usually smart. It's obvious he spends a lot of time on his grooming. Down to earth, he's never boasting or trying to impress.

He gives the appearance of an honest young lad looking to improve his life. He's very open and told me his mother is an alcoholic, and his father left home when he was only six.

He has an older sister and two older brothers, but none of them works or contributes anything to his life.

Freddie's a trainee. His duties cover everything from unblocking the toilets to moving beds and furniture. I've noticed he often works extra time after his shift.

It's easy to like Freddie, but I hope someone tells him he smells like a chimney (in the nicest way of course). If he can give up smoking, I'm sure his chances of advancing his career will be greatly improved.

I like him a lot, except for the stench of nicotine.

CHAPTER FORTY-FIVE

JAMES

As I walk through the front entrance of the Albion, I'm happy to see George standing by the reception desk. He's chatting with Belinda Grant, the part-time receptionist. It's obvious he has a soft spot for her. When I've seen them together, they're always laughing and smiling at each other.

As I approach, George turns and looks at me. At first, he's not sure who I am, but then, to my amazement, he recognises me.

"Hello, my friend. Well, you certainly look much better than last time I saw you. Welcome to the Albion Hotel. I guess these days you can afford to walk in the front door. Have you come to stay in one of the rooms, or do you want your old suite back?" He grins.

His last comment brings a big smile to my face. "I'm not sure I can afford the prices here."

He laughs.

"It's great to see you, George. I wonder if we could have a little chat – could we sit in the bar and have a drink?"

"I'll take a coffee with you if that's okay?" he says as we walk through.

The bar also acts as a coffee lounge. It consists of a dozen circular tables with four brown leather chairs around each. We find a secluded table, which isn't difficult as only three other tables are taken.

The waitress comes over, and I recognise Stella. She says hello and asks what we would like.

George orders a cappuccino, and I opt for a latte.

"Look, George, I came here today to tell you how much the sleeping quarters out back helped. I noticed the things you did for me. I want to thank you for your kindness and say, from the bottom of my heart, that I appreciate everything you did."

He looks at me, and, from his expression, I can tell he doesn't have a clue what I'm about to do.

"When I needed somewhere, a place I could feel relatively safe, your acts of kindness went above and beyond. So now it's my turn to do the same for you.

"I've done some checking. A three-bedroom house in Trentbridge is around one hundred and seventy thousand pounds. On top of that, it will cost an extra ten thousand to furnish it.

"So, I've decided to round it up a little – why not have a nice holiday as well? Take someone with you – maybe Belinda needs a break? Anyway, I'd like you to accept this cheque for two hundred thousand pounds as the only way I can thank you. I'm so happy to be in a position where I can repay your kindness. It means I'm going to get even more pleasure out of this than you are."

George looks me squarely in the eyes, and I can see tears forming. He remains speechless for a few seconds. Stella comes over with our coffees. She sees the state he's in and looks concerned.

"What's the matter, George? Is something wrong?"

"No, Stella, nothing's wrong. It's just this man's act of kindness has caught me off guard."

Stella gives him a big smile and places the coffees on the table. Her concern surprises me. She's always seemed a bit of a tough cookie. It seems I don't know her as well as I thought. Even an ex-detective can get it wrong sometimes.

George takes a few seconds to compose himself. I can see from his face that he's trying to take it all in. I know that feeling from when I discovered I'd won the Lotto.

After a few seconds, his gaze comes back to me.

"This means so much. I can get a place of my own. It's a dream come true. If there's anything I can do in the future to thank you, let me know."

I beam at his words. "I'm glad you're pleased. Being able to do this for you, that's my reward. Now I wonder if you *could* do me a favour. Is young Freddie working at the moment? He always treated me well, so would it be possible to have a word with him?"

"Yes. He's a nice lad and a hard worker," says George. He tells me that he's sure Freddie's around and goes off to try to find him.

After a couple of minutes, I see them coming back.

"Hello, Freddie. Please have a seat. I'm not sure if George has told you, but I'm the guy who used to sleep out the back. From time to time, you'd come and talk to me on your ciggie breaks."

Freddie gasps then smiles. "Yes, I remember you, but you look a lot different now. I heard about your big win. It's been the talk of everyone here."

"Would you like a coffee or something to drink?"

"No, I'm fine."

He looks a little awkward, uncertain of what this is all about. I decide not to keep him guessing.

"Freddie, I remember your kindness towards me, so I'd like to thank you in a way which, I hope, shows my appreciation." With that, I hand him an envelope. He opens it, and I can see the unexpected joy on his face as he reads his name and 'fifteen thousand pounds' written on a cheque.

"Bloomin' 'eck! That's more than I get in a year. I didn't expect this."

"How could you? I'm still taking it in myself, but one thing's for sure; the money I won is going to be put to good use. I have plans to ensure it helps a lot of deserving people, and you're one of them."

Freddie gives me a big hug and keeps saying "Thank you." I tell him he should take his break and go and pay in the cheque at the bank.

Stella comes over to enquire if we need anything, and I ask her for the bill.

It comes to six pounds twenty. I leave her a twenty-pound note.

CHAPTER FORTY-SIX

DAVE

Wednesday 2nd November 2016

The motorway is quiet as Dave Rex drives home from the airport. After two weeks of glorious sunshine, he feels the cold. He's got the car air-conditioning blasting out at twenty-five degrees. He drives to his luxury apartment at Brampton Manor, walking through the front door at nine forty-five p.m.

He picks up the pile of letters his cleaner has left on the hall table and strolls into the kitchen. With a flick of a switch, the coffee machine spurts into life. Once it has done its work, he sits down to catch up with the stack of mail.

There's nothing to warrant his urgent attention: a few bills, which his accountant can deal with, and a couple of pieces of junk mail.

His first thought is to see how his favourite football team is doing. He's been a fan of Trentbridge Rovers since he was a kid and went to matches with his dad. Dave picks up the latest issue of the local free newspaper that's delivered every week. He looks at the back page and sees they drew 2–2.

He then picks up the previous issue and turns to the back page. He's chuffed to read 'The Rovers Thrash Peterborough 4–1.' Then he remembers he hasn't checked his Euro Lotto ticket from the day he went on holiday. He skips back six pages to where he knows the Lotto results are listed.

He becomes more excited as he goes through the numbers one by one. He doesn't want to believe what he is seeing until he has found his ticket, but the winning numbers appear very familiar.

Being a creature of habit, he knows the ticket will be in his desk drawer: the second down on the left. The place he empties the contents of his pockets every evening. The last time he did this was two weeks ago before he took his mum her present.

He sits on his Herman Miller Aeron executive chair and places the ticket on the desk next to the newspaper. Slowly, the grin on his face starts to disappear. He doesn't recognise the numbers on the ticket. It doesn't take him long to realise this is not his ticket. At least not the one he remembers filling out at the convenience store two weeks ago. He tries to recall if he went for a lucky dip in the rush? But he is pretty sure he used his regular numbers.

He turns the newspaper over to check the date and make sure it's from the week he went on holiday. As he does, he reads the front-page headline: 'Local Homeless Man Wins £168 Million Lotto'.

He sees the photo of the winner. Then it dawns on him: the 'human piece of crap' he collided with in the shop. He remembers his ticket slipped from his grasp for a few seconds. It was when they both fell to the floor. Could the tickets have got mixed up?

Dave's anger quickly rises to boiling point. He screams

out a massive "Arrgggh!" before using a torrent of four-letter words.

He paces the room before moving back through to the lounge. He grabs the bottle of Jack Daniel's, his favourite tipple. He pours himself a large glass and downs the contents in one gulp. He resists the urge to fling the glass across the room.

A man on a mission, he picks up his car keys and heads for the door.

Ten minutes later, he arrives at Tindall's Convenience Store on Market Street, the place where he purchased what he is convinced was the winning ticket. Dave speaks to the young girl assistant in such a rough tone that she immediately calls the night-time manager, who joins them.

"Hello, sir. How can I help you?"

"I bought a Lotto ticket two weeks ago. The one that won the one hundred and sixty-eight million, and some dirty tramp nicked it from me. I know you have security cameras. I need to see them so I can get my money."

"Two weeks ago, you say. That's a problem, sir. We don't keep the security tapes for more than a week. They're automatically recorded over after seven days, so we wouldn't have the footage anymore."

Standing in a corner at the back of the shop, Dave is in no mood for a reply that includes the word 'no'.

"Look, you prat. I need those pictures. I don't care what you have to do, but I'm warning you..." Dave grabs the manager's shirt collar and pulls him forward. "Get me those bloody tapes or there's gonna be trouble!"

"I... I can't, sir. As I told you, we don't keep the tapes that long. The system's not that sophisticated. I'd love to help you but—"

"Don't give me that. There has to be a way."

The man pulls back. "I... I really can't help you, sir. I'm sorry. If there was anything I could do—"

Dave grabs the man's shirt again and is about to land a punch. He changes his mind when he remembers the CCTV cameras. He looks up and sees one pointing directly to where he's standing. He drops his hold and starts to walk away.

Turning back, Dave barks at the manager. "Don't think you've heard the last of this, you prat. You'll be hearing from my lawyers. I'll sodding 'ave you, you bastard."

Dave has been a career criminal for over thirty years, but he's never actually killed anyone himself. However, right now, should anyone cross him, he might do something he could regret. He will find the little shit who robbed him and make sure he pays.

Even though it's close to eleven p.m., he decides to go looking for anyone who might know the man who stole his winning ticket. He's seen the doorways where the homeless people sit and beg for money. So he walks around to West Street, leaving his car in a disabled parking bay.

Dave searches every shop doorway for someone who might be homeless. He wants to discover the identity of the man who, he has decided, will come to a sticky end. That is, once Dave grabs back his winning ticket.

Unable to find anyone, he decides to cut his losses and

return home. Tomorrow is another day, and he'll get everything sorted if it's the last thing he does.

Dave returns home and pours himself a large Jack Daniel's. He takes a big gulp and mutters, through gritted teeth, "Tomorrow, I'll find the bastard and tear him limb from limb."

CHAPTER FORTY-SEVEN

JAMES

Wednesday 2nd November 2016

I walk into my hotel's restaurant for breakfast. As I look around for an empty table, I notice a stand holding a stack of the local newspaper. There's a sign saying, 'Please Take Your Free Copy.'

I've already decided to spend the day looking for a house to buy, so I grab a paper and turn to the property section. All I want is something in a quiet location with a decent-sized garden. I'm not looking for anything fancy or too expensive.

I draw a circle around one of the listings. It's a three-bedroom detached at a reasonable price, located on the edge of town, away from other people. That's exactly what I'm looking for.

Then I notice an article saying the council is planning to sell off the run-down estate known as Asbury Park. The property I'm interested in is close by. Both are on the other side of the River Stern.

I glance at the article with details of the estate. In total, there are eight hundred and eighty houses. It states that the houses and road surfaces require extensive improvement. It also includes a large area of land with commercial opportunities.

This could be the project I've been looking for. Maybe I can help deserving families find a decent home.

The article goes on to say the council is looking for sealed-bid offers. I'm not sure what that will entail, but it shouldn't be too hard to find out.

Right now though, my priority is to find somewhere to call my own. I don't want to live in a hotel, tempting as it might seem. I think I'll try to view that house.

I start the ten-minute journey from the Premier Inn to Millers Estate Agents; I walk down Rosslyn Road and across to Harper Street, where most of the estate agents in town are, passing several of Millers' competitors on my way to their shop at number 69. When I get there, I look at all the properties in the window and spot the one I'm looking for.

As I enter, one of the staff members stands from behind his desk. The man looks to be in his late fifties, medium height, with silver hair and wearing a light-grey suit. Within seconds he's greeting me with a warm handshake.

"Good morning. I'm Daniel Miller. How can I help you today?"

"Hi, Daniel. I'm looking at the property you have over on Foundry Road, on the edge of Asbury Park. Is it possible to arrange a viewing?"

"Yes, of course. I've got an appointment over that way later today if that's not too soon?"

"No. That suits me. Could we say two thirty?"

"I'll meet you there, on the dot. In the meantime, could I take some details please?"

After a further brief chat and another warm handshake, Daniel returns to his desk, and I walk back out onto the street.

It's eleven a.m., and I decide it would be a good idea to buy a mobile phone; the last one I had was the property of the local police force, so I could be on call twenty-four hours a day. I walk to the Phone Superstore on the high street, where I'm greeted by a young guy. He shows me the latest models and explains the options. I decide on the new Samsung.

Getting to the Asbury Park estate from the town centre is not easy. By car or taxi, it's at least a twenty-five-minute journey. You have to go around the River Stern via the main road out to Stonebridge. The 104 bus takes around forty-five minutes. They only run once every three hours, but there's an alternative.

The 42 bus goes to Pickstone and takes about ten minutes. Then I'll be able to cross the pedestrian-only footbridge over the river, followed by a five-minute walk along Trentbridge Road to Foundry Road and eventually the Asbury Park estate.

There's a bus stop outside the main post office on Morley Street, and I join the short queue.

After a ten-minute wait, I see the bus approaching: a green single-decker and it's on time, which is nice. I pay the one-pound-twenty fare to Pickstone High Street and sit about halfway along, on the driver's side of the bus.

My fellow passengers are a mixed bunch. Two ladies, who look to be in their seventies, sit at the front of the bus, gleefully chatting away.

There's a young mother in her mid-twenties. Sitting next to her, and holding her hand, is a girl of around five. The young lady also has a buggy, with what looks like a one-year-old baby.

In the back row are two young men dressed in Superdry sweatshirts and jeans. They seem to be around thirteen and I'd guess they're playing truant from school.

Sitting behind me is a man who looks to be in his forties; he's very overweight and short. In the row opposite sits a young lady, spending all her time texting.

We set off, and I soon understand why he's unlikely to win 'Driver of the Year'. He doesn't wait for people to sit before he races off. One lady nearly falls over as he pulls away the moment she's paid her fare.

I wait my turn behind the two elderly ladies and the young mum before getting off the bus at Pickstone High Street. The bus speeds away the moment my foot hits the pavement.

I'm feeling a little peckish. It's a sensation I'd forgotten about, which has only returned since my change of fortune. When you're homeless, you learn not to think about regular meals. It's as though your hunger system turns itself off.

I soon notice the reason for my sudden urge to eat. I can see – smell actually – a local branch of Greggs the bakers, two doors down. I study the menu displayed on the wall and order a toasted cheese sandwich and a cup of tea.

Ten minutes later and I've finished. The restaurant is starting to get busy; most of the tables are occupied, so I vacate mine to allow someone else to use it.

Upon leaving, I turn left along the high street. I want to get a feel for the area. It also helps to fill some time until my appointment. I walk past two second-hand shops. Both have a display of used furniture and household goods spilling out onto the pavement.

Just by Bernard Isaacks Pharmacy, I cross at the pedestrian crossing. A few doors down I pass the pawnbrokers on the corner of Lonsdale Road. Outside is a large sign offering to buy unwanted gold and jewellery.

At the junction, I check nothing's coming, then head further down. The number of shoppers seems to be decreasing, presumably because most of the shops this far down are vacant.

Just before the end of the shopping parade, I notice the young woman from the bus, with her two children. She's looking in the window of a shoe shop with her back to me. She speaks to the older child. "I'm sorry, Daisy. I know you need new shoes, but Mummy can't afford them at the moment. I promise I'll get some for you soon."

By this time, I'm standing behind her, pretending to look in the shop window. She's busy with her two children and hasn't noticed me. I place my hand into my trouser pocket, where I know I have two fifty-pound notes. I pull one of them out and drop the note to the ground, before I turn to her and say, in a clear voice, "Excuse me, miss. I think you've dropped something." I point to the note.

She turns, looks at me, then to where I'm pointing. "It's not mine," she tells me.

"It certainly isn't mine, and it's right where you've been standing. I don't see anyone else around, so I'm sure it belongs to you. Perhaps you forgot you were saving up."

With the instinct of a mother looking out for her children, she seems to read the message in my eyes.

"God bless you," she says with genuine gratitude.

"And you."

As I walk away, it's gratifying to hear her say, "Today's our lucky day, Daisy. Which pair would you like?"

CHAPTER FORTY-EIGHT

JAMES

I arrive a few minutes early for my appointment with Daniel Miller. I sit on the low brick wall at the front of the house. To pass the time, I pull out the section of the newspaper where I saw the listing.

As I flick through, I notice an article about the history of Asbury Park. It informs me that it started life as Asbury Farm. Then the land was purchased by an industrialist who built the Asbury Iron Foundry in 1866.

The original road that led to the farm was a tiny hamlet which consisted of four farm workers' cottages.

The foundry grew over the years. At some point during the 1930s, the company tore down the dilapidated cottages. In their place, they built thirty-two semi-detached three-bedroom houses. These were for their key people. Then someone with a lack of imagination came up with the name Foundry Road.

According to the article, in its heyday, the foundry was one of the largest employers in the area. To attract local workers, they built a bridge across the river, creating a direct route to the town.

At the outbreak of World War Two, it started making equipment for the war effort. One night in May 1941, the German Luftwaffe targeted the foundry. Sixteen aircraft opened their bomb doors as they circled above. They dropped two hundred and sixty tonnes of high explosives onto the foundry and the bridge. The attack was over in less than twenty minutes.

The newspaper interviewed a lady, now well into her nineties. She still recalls *the night the bombs rained down and the bridge was blown to smithereens.*

The article goes on to say that the air raid claimed the lives of two hundred and twenty-four people and caused significant damage to the foundry. There are black-and-white photos of the foundry before the attack, and the destruction left behind.

The war ended in 1945, and the foundry closed the following year. Without the bridge, it became a remote place.

I put down the newspaper and glance at my phone.

Right on time, Daniel pulls up. He parks on the other side of the road, gets out, locks the car, and walks over to greet me, his hand outstretched.

I thank him for being punctual.

"No problem," he replies, unlocking the front door of the house. "Shall we go inside?"

I step onto the deep pile hall carpet and glance at the decoration on the walls. It all looks immaculate. The previous owner must have been a skilled craftsman.

With his next comment, Daniel confirms it. "As you can see, it's in lovely condition."

"The previous owner was a retired builder with time on

his hands. He took a lot of pride in the appearance of his home. Sadly, he had to be taken into a nursing home and passed away a few weeks ago. His family wants a quick sale, hence the low asking price."

I look around the living room, the kitchen and finally, the three bedrooms upstairs. Two are quite big. The third is smaller but still large enough to use as a home office, or I could put in some gym equipment. I know I need to get fit again.

Daniel starts his sales pitch. "These were built in the 1930s. The rooms are a good size; there's central heating, double glazing and a decent garden. The walls are quite solid, unlike the ones developers build today."

I look out the back bedroom window at the hundred-foot-long well-kept garden. The house looks perfect and has a pleasant atmosphere about it. I feel at home already.

"So, what do you think of the house?" asks Daniel, hopefully.

"I like it, and, subject to a survey, I'd like to put in an offer. I'm a cash buyer, so how soon can we get things underway?"

"I'll speak with the seller today and contact you as soon as I receive a reply."

Once we're back outside, Daniel asks if I'd like a lift to Trentbridge. I tell him I'm fine, so we shake hands, and he gets into his car and drives off.

The time is a little after three so I decide, while I'm here, it's a good opportunity to walk along to Asbury Park. I'll take a quick look at the houses the council are planning to sell off.

The bus schedule means I don't have enough time to see them all. The ones I do have a chance to view look fine from the outside. And the gardens seem to be a generous size.

Especially when you compare them to the tiny patches you get with newbuild houses. With some of them, if your hobby is swinging cats, you could be out of luck!

The houses I've seen on Asbury Park remind me of the big house we lived in before Dad lost his job and we had to move. I remember how lovely it was to have a garden to play in.

I walk back along Foundry Road to the pedestrian-only bridge and cross back over to Pickstone High Street.

Waiting at the bus stop, I see a bicycle shop across the road. A bike would be a good way of getting back into shape. It could be useful if my offer on the house is accepted.

As I wait for the bus to arrive, ideas run through my head. The Asbury Park estate could house a great many deserving families. I'm beginning to think I've discovered the perfect way to use the money I've won.

And I have someone in mind who might be able to assist me.

CHAPTER FORTY-NINE

JAMES

The bus was late, so it's now four-fifteen, and I have one more place to visit. Arriving at the library on Lockwood Road, I walk in and see Miss Hartman standing behind the counter. There are two other people in the library. Both are busy choosing books, so I walk over to the reception desk.

"Hello. Remember me?" I smile at her.

There's a puzzled look on her face, and it takes her a few seconds to work out who I am. She smiles. "My, you look much better than the last time I saw you. How are you doing?"

"I'm fine. Thank you for all your help."

"It was my pleasure. So, how can I help you today?"

"I want to use some of the money I've won to form a housing trust charity. I was hoping you might be able to offer me some advice?"

"That sounds like a wonderful idea. It's a little difficult to discuss things here. It might be better if we meet up somewhere, then you can tell me more about your ideas, and I can tell you how I can help."

"Perhaps we could chat over a meal? It would be my treat, of course!"

"When did you have in mind?"

"How does tonight work?"

"I can't make it tonight, but I'm free tomorrow."

"Okay. What time suits?"

"The library closes at six. If I pop home first, I can meet you at, say, seven thirty?"

"Okay. I'll book a table. I was thinking of going to Marloes on Etruria Road, what do you think?"

"That's a splendid choice. I'll meet you there tomorrow. Sorry, must get on."

"Yes, of course. Tomorrow at seven thirty."

With that, Miss Hartman turns to a lady waiting to take out three books.

As I arrive back in my room at the Premier Inn, my mobile rings. I know it's the estate agent. He's the only person I've given the number to.

"Hello, Mr Sheldon. It's Daniel Miller. I'm delighted to say your offer on 27 Foundry Road has been accepted. The party concerned is happy to go ahead as soon as possible."

"Thanks for letting me know, Daniel. I have the money in place and the name of a conveyancing lawyer. I'll phone him tomorrow and get things underway."

CHAPTER FIFTY

DAVE

Thursday 3rd November 2016

"Good morning – Curtis, Jackson, and Dean."

"Let me speak with Mark Jackson," growls a voice on the other end of the phone.

"I'm sorry, but Mr Jackson won't be in the office until nine-fifteen."

"Then get him to phone Dave Rex the instant he gets in," the voice demands.

"Certainly, sir," Katie, the receptionist, replies. She's well-versed in dealing with stroppy clients. "Does he have your phone number?"

"Yes. Make sure he calls me without delay." With that, the line goes dead.

Ten minutes later, Mark Jackson walks into reception. He and Katie exchange their usual morning pleasantries. Katie hands him a written note with the message to call Dave Rex urgently.

Once seated behind his desk, Mark consults his diary. His first appointment isn't until ten, so he has time to make the call. Before he can lift the receiver though, the phone rings.

"Hello, Mr Jackson," says Katie. "I have Dave Rex on the phone again for you."

"Okay, Katie. Put him through."

"Mark!" the voice bellows. "I've been cheated out of a fortune. I need you to take care of it for me. The bastard has robbed me. I'm talking about millions. I want justice. I want him thrown in jail."

"Calm down, Dave. Perhaps you could start at the beginning. Explain the situation so I can advise you accordingly."

Mark listens to the story of how Dave believes the Lotto tickets became mixed up. Dave tells him how this homeless bum is now living the life of Riley with his money.

Mark listens and advises his client that the best way to deal with this is through the courts. He's aware of his client's reputation. He knows that if Dave decides to take matters into his own hands, the other person could end up in hospital, or worse.

That means his client would be facing serious criminal charges or even a murder charge. But, in the back of his mind, Mark's not sure Dave is listening to a word he's saying. Whoever this person is, Mark wouldn't like to be in his shoes when Dave Rex catches up with him.

CHAPTER FIFTY-ONE

JAMES

Thursday 3rd November 2016

I'm already sitting in the restaurant when Miss Hartman walks in. She looks around, sees me, waves and walks over.

The wine waiter arrives. We opt for sparkling water.

We order the first course. While we're waiting, we chat about things in general and touch on the subject of the Lotto win.

Finally, Miss Hartman asks, "So, tell me what you have in mind."

I reach down beside my chair, bring up a yellow document wallet and take out two sheets of paper.

"I've brought some plans to show you. I'm thinking about buying the old Asbury Park council properties. I'd like to restore them and rent them out at a reasonable cost. I'm thinking they could be perfect for homeless people, and families who are currently in expensive private housing."

I take a quick sip of my water then continue. "I need a

logical thinker to help me put everything in place. As you know, I've been coming to the library for years. In my opinion, you're the best person to help me do this. I have to say, ideally, you'd be able to come in full-time. But I realise you're dedicated to your career."

Miss Hartman, listening intently, smiles. "There's something I should mention. The council is closing the library. They say government cutbacks mean they can't afford to keep it open, and they're selling off the land to developers. When it goes ahead, I'll be made redundant. So perhaps this has come at a fortuitous time for both of us."

"That's so sad about the library but incredible for me. You've got the job. When can you start?" I raise an eyebrow.

We laugh. The waiter reappears holding two plates, with the aroma of food cooked to perfection.

"By the way," says Miss Hartman, "please call me Susan."

After letting dessert go down, we sit and enjoy our cups of coffee.

"So now you've had a chance to see the plans, I'd be grateful for your feedback."

"It's a very bold plan, but if you can pull it off, many families will be able to enjoy living there." She looks up. "Houses with gardens, just what people need."

After our meal, Miss Hartman, sorry, Susan, says we should discuss the matter in more detail.

She invites me to visit her at home the following evening and writes down her address, handing me the slip of paper.

"14 Pemberton Avenue. Do you know where that is?"

"I do. I didn't realise you lived around there."

"When you come over, I'll tell you a few things about a poor librarian that you probably didn't realise."

With Susan's help, it all sounds like it's going to be a piece of cake! With millions in the bank and a lady with her background, it's the perfect combination.

What can possibly go wrong?

CHAPTER FIFTY-TWO

DAVE

Friday 4th November 2016

Dave has been on the phone to the Lotto company. The person on the other end remained courteous despite Dave's shouting and swearing, and managed to tell him they were not prepared to get involved without proof.

Dave's lawyer has taken advice from two high-ranking barristers. They have both advised he might have a case. Their fees range between eight hundred and one thousand pounds per hour. And it's entirely possible the case could drag on for months. So the legal bill could be in excess of a million pounds, but they do state that, in their opinion, he has a good chance of winning.

Dave's had several encounters with lawyers and barristers throughout his chequered past. He knows they often say you have a strong case until instructed to proceed. Then, gradually, they don't seem to offer as much reassurance. He's not daft. He understands it's in their interest to get the case started. They won't lose whichever way the court decides.

He's also thinking of alternative ways to recoup his money. In his opinion, this homeless tramp needs to be taught the lesson of his life.

Dave's first thought is to hire the two Albanians again and have the bum killed. However, as pleasing as this might be, it won't lead to him getting his hands on whatever's left of the money after the bastard's likely spending spree.

If the only outcome is to torture and murder the bum, then Dave might enjoy it. In fact, the more he thinks about it, the more he likes the idea. Or perhaps he'll have him bumped off after he gets his hands on the money. Yes, that would be perfect. That's what he'll do. The bum will meet with a fatal accident.

But first, he needs to find out all he can about the good-for-nothing arsehole living off his winnings.

CHAPTER FIFTY-THREE

JAMES

Friday 4th November 2016

At half past seven, the taxi turns into the driveway of 14 Pemberton Avenue. It's a large detached house on one of the better roads in the Cherrywood area. *I didn't think a librarian's salary could stretch to this.*

I ring the front doorbell and wait. After a few seconds, Susan answers, and I'm invited in. She shows me through to the tastefully decorated living room. The centrepiece is a cream leather sofa with two matching recliners in a U shape. Set in front is a solid oak Ercol coffee table.

On the facing wall is a large flat-screen TV. The far side of the room has a long section of floor-to-ceiling bookshelves, as you might expect from a librarian. The other two walls have a range of modern art paintings by artists I'm unfamiliar with. Mind you, I couldn't tell a Picasso from a Pollock. I can, however, spot good taste when it's staring me in the face, and Susan has more than her fair share.

It looks like a lot of thought has gone into the layout and

furnishings. The lighting in the room is modern and bright, but not overly glaring. The whole atmosphere is high-end and contemporary.

I'm brought back to earth when Susan asks, "What would you like to drink?"

"A glass of water for me."

"Please, make yourself comfortable." Susan points towards one of the chairs. She disappears in the direction of the kitchen, before returning and handing me a tall thin glass. "The food will be ready shortly."

She sits down on the chair opposite me.

"When we spoke in the restaurant, I told you there was a little more to me than you knew. For a start, I'm sure you're wondering how I can afford to live in a large house like this. My father was a successful property developer. When he died, I inherited this house plus his property portfolio.

"My first love has always been books, and I had the good fortune to be educated at a private school. I then went to Oxford University. For the past twelve years, in my spare time, I've been helping out at a couple of local voluntary organisations for families with housing problems. So, you see, I might be able to help you in more ways than you thought."

She stands. "The food should be ready now. Let's go through to the dining room. I hope you're hungry."

Susan brings two plates through and places mine in front of me.

"Mmmm, spaghetti Bolognese. It's been a long time since I've had that."

After the food is out of the way, we clear the dining room table. Susan wipes it clean then spreads out several sheets of paper. "I did some research of my own. It seems the council have tried to sell Asbury Park a few times over the years, but no developer has been prepared to take it on.

"They've all been put off by the amount of repair the houses need. Then there's the cost of rebuilding the bridge, and the road structure to connect it with the town centre, and that's before you've even looked at the state of its internal roads.

"Younger families don't want to live there because there's no broadband and they can't get a signal on their mobile. And all the elderly people moved out after the approach road kept getting flooded, leading to ambulance delays. Four people died from heart attacks while they were waiting for treatment. The place has been left to rot.

"But it has so much potential. If you're as dedicated as you seem, then I'll help you as much as I can. And you certainly have the money."

"That's wonderful news, Susan. Yes, I'm totally serious. The money I won means very little to me. If it can be used to help other people, then I'm all for it."

"In that case, I know a lawyer who specialises in setting up charitable foundations. He can make sure everything's done correctly. All we have to do is come up with a detailed plan and put in a bid to the council."

CHAPTER FIFTY-FOUR

PHIL JONES

Monday 7th November 2016

Ex-police detective-turned-private investigator Phil Jones checks his voicemail messages. Today there is only one. It's from someone called Dave Rex. The only person he can recall with that name is someone he remembers seeing in police files.

That was during his time as a serving police detective, although he had no direct dealings with the man. If it is him, why would he be calling? Still, business is business. "Hello. This is Phil Jones Private Investigations. You left a message?"

"Yeah, that's right. I need some background info on someone, and you come recommended."

"Okay. Who's the person in question, and what sort of information do you need?"

"His name's Anthony Sheldon. He's the tramp who's supposed to have won the Lotto. I want to know everything about his past and where he's living now."

"Do you have anything for me to go on?"

"A newspaper cutting, but that's about it. Listen, this man stole my Lotto ticket and has claimed the money that's rightfully mine. I want the background on him for my lawyer, Mark Jackson. He's the one who recommended you."

"Okay. My fees for this type of work are four hundred pounds a day plus expenses. I should be able to find all the information you need in a couple of days, depending on my initial findings. If that's acceptable, subject to an upfront payment, I can get started today."

"That's agreed then. I can send you the newspaper cutting, then I'll wait to hear from you. Remember – I want everything on this guy. From when he was born to where he's living now."

"Okay. If I give you my email address, can you send over what you've got so far?"

"I'm not great with computers, I try to avoid them if I can, so no, I can't. I'll get someone to drop it off to you within the hour. And I'll send the money over in cash."

Phil doesn't need the newspaper cutting. He remembers the article, because he recognised James. The pair used to be friends as well as colleagues. So, it's best he carries out this work in the hope he can discover what's going on. Then, if he needs to, he can get word to his old mate.

Within the hour, a taxi arrives at Phil's house.

"Mr Rex asked me to drop this off to you." The driver hands over a sealed jiffy bag.

"Wait there while I check this."

Phil walks to his office and counts the cash. He sees the newspaper cutting and the note attached with Dave's address and phone number. He returns to the front door and hands the driver an envelope addressed to Dave Rex. It contains a receipt for the payment.

Armed with these details, Phil makes a call. Like most private investigators, he doesn't carry out this sort of work himself. Within the PI industry, there are small companies that undertake this sort of research for a fee. Phil will then charge his client twice the price and pocket the difference.

CHAPTER FIFTY-FIVE

JAMES

Wednesday 9th November 2016

I know it's only been three weeks since I won the Lotto, but I'm anxious to move ahead with my plans for the charity. I've rented two first-floor offices at a shared business complex on West Street, just along the road from the doorway I used to sit in. The main office is large and has space for up to eight people to work comfortably.

The second office is far smaller and solely for my use. Although I'll spend most of my time in the main office, this is a place I can sit on my own when I need to.

My recent visit to a local tech showroom means we have a network of computers and printers. And a local office furniture company have delivered desks, bookcases and filing cabinets.

It's a bold move to rent offices before even winning the bid, but we must show people we're serious. If we're not able to buy Asbury Park, then we'll need to consider an alternative. I've been in touch with several estate agents and requested details of the properties they have for sale. One way or another, I'm determined to use this money to help people.

Susan suggested we recruit an experienced office manager who can keep everything running smoothly on a day-to-day basis. We were lucky enough to find Fiona Dean, a lady in her mid-thirties, with shoulder-length blonde hair.

Fiona stood out above the other candidates. In the two days she's worked here, she's already added plants and large prints to decorate the walls. It's made the place a pleasant, friendly and inviting environment.

Fiona is such a happy person. The office is filled with her pleasant perfume, although I couldn't tell you the name of it. And she certainly knows how to organise. Everything down to the last paperclip has its place.

I've also found a two-bedroom apartment to rent at a small complex called Meadowcroft on Keele Street. I'll stay there until the purchase of Foundry Road goes through. The apartment's only a mile from the town centre, so, weather permitting, I can ride into the office on my new bicycle. I spent a small fortune on a bike lock – you can't be too careful.

I've also bought myself a car, a two-year-old Ford Mondeo. I've no need for a fancy one. Maybe I'll splash out on a luxury sports car in the future, but for now, the charity is my main focus.

CHAPTER FIFTY-SIX

PHIL

Wednesday 9th November 2016

It's been two days since Phil Jones received instructions from his client. He now has a detailed dossier. He calls Dave Rex and arranges to go and see him at his home.

Arriving on time, Phil is disappointed not to be offered a coffee. He can see his client is anxious to learn what he has discovered.

"This is what I have so far: James Anthony Sheldon, born on the 7th July 1982, in Surbiton, Surrey. When he was eight, his parents moved to Trentbridge. He did very well at school and achieved good grades, gaining a place at Manchester University. It seems he was always interested in joining the police force and did so shortly after leaving university."

"What!" exclaims Dave. "So, he's a bloody rozzer, and he steals my money? You can't trust anyone these days."

Phil Jones pauses for a couple of seconds.

"He married Miriam Shepherd in August 2008, when he was twenty-six, and she was twenty-five. They had two children: a son called Jack and a daughter, Abigail. His police career went well; he was due to be promoted to detective inspector in June last year. Sadly, a couple of weeks before that could happen, his wife and two children were killed in a hit-and-run."

Dave sits straight up. "Hang on a minute – what did you say this guy's name was?"

"James Sheldon." Jones wonders why Dave has gone pale.

"But the papers called him Anthony?"

"Yes, but they got that wrong. His full name is James Anthony Sheldon."

"And he was in the police, you say?"

"Yes, as I explained, he was due to be promoted to detective inspector. By all accounts, he was an outstanding police officer. No reports or complaints on his record." Phil deliberately makes no mention of his own connection to James.

Dave flops back in his chair, shaking his head and muttering, "That guy. Of all the bums, it could have been... that guy."

Phil waits for Dave to compose himself before continuing. "Apparently, he went to pieces after his wife and kids were killed. His house was repossessed by the building society, and he became homeless. He seems to have been living rough until about three weeks ago. Then, as you read in the newspaper, he won the Lotto, with the ticket you say was yours," Phil is careful to add.

"He doesn't have any living family, estranged from his in-laws, so I understand. His parents are both deceased, and he was an only child. People I have spoken to tell me the experience turned him to religion. He's been a regular at St Matthew's Church. Do you want me to keep digging, although I'm not sure what more you'd need to know?"

"Do you have a current address for him?"

"Yes. It's all in the file. He's staying at the Premier Inn on Etruria Road."

"Okay. You've done a good job."

Phil says goodbye to Dave Rex and walks to the car park. He gets into his car and drives off.

Phil parks his car ready for his next appointment. He searches the directory on his phone. He finds the number for Detective Chief Inspector Andy Stone and presses connect.

"Hello, Phil. Haven't heard from you recently. Do you need another favour?"

"Hi, Andy, not today. I wanted to pass something on to you in confidence. I've been hired by someone we crossed paths with. Do you remember Dave Rex?"

"Gosh, you're going back a bit. Yes, I recall. We never did manage to get anything on the little toerag. As far as we know, he hasn't been active for years. Is he up to something?"

"Possibly. I don't have any details. But he asked me to get background on someone we both know – James Anthony Sheldon."

"Blimey. Why would he want background info on James? I read something about him winning some money on the lottery, but why the interest?"

"From the tone of things, it's not to congratulate him on

his win. He seems to think James stole the ticket from him. It sounds crazy, but I thought you might want to warn James. He was a good lad before the family tragedy. I wouldn't want to see him come to any harm due to Mr Rex or his associates."

"Thanks, Phil. Let me think about it, and I'll decide on the best thing to do. Let me know if you hear anything else."

"Will do. All the best, and say *hello* to Sheila for me."

After thirty years in the police force, Phil Jones knows who the good guys are and who not to trust. Andy Stone and James Sheldon are most definitely good guys. He certainly doesn't want to see any harm come to James because of someone like Dave Rex.

Phil walks into the Red Brick Café, where he's arranged to meet a client who thinks her husband is cheating on her. He looks at his watch: ten minutes early. He orders a cappuccino, sits down, and starts to think about his old CID buddies. This was their favourite meeting place.

DCI Larry Archer, DCI Gerry Payne, DS James Sheldon, and Phil: people called them the Fab Four because, between them, they solved more crimes than anyone else in the division. Phil wonders if he should consider organising a catch-up. Something for old times' sake?

It's such a shame about Larry. In two or three weeks, it'll be six years to the day.

Phil thinks back to what little he knows: Larry received a phone call. As he left his office, he told a junior female colleague he was on his way to meet a potential whistle-blower in the council fraud case he was working on. He walked out of the police station and vanished.

After all this time, they would probably never find out what happened to him.

It still jarred, one of the few major crimes they'd never been able to solve.

CHAPTER FIFTY-SEVEN

JAMES

Friday 11th November 2016

This morning, Susan and I visited the Asbury Park estate. We spent two hours with two local building contractors and a surveyor examining the condition of the houses.

One of the contractors seemed to know a great deal about the area.

"I remember when it was built in the late 1970s. The council was run by a gentleman called Jasper Kriss. In my opinion, he was quite a visionary. He could see the potential of quality homes for ordinary people, so he set up a project to regenerate the area.

"The council built eight hundred and eighty houses plus a handful of industrial units. All it needed was the bridge to connect it with the town. But when the recession of the early eighties kicked in, some council members said it was throwing good money after bad and the work was put on hold.

"I heard Jasper found some private investors willing to

put up the money. Then he was killed in a freak accident, and, without his vision, everything came to a halt, meaning vehicles have to take the road out of Pickstone, to the end of Old Quarry Road, then round the other side of the river. It's a fifteen-mile journey.

"It only took us twenty-five minutes to get here today, luckily. But when Trentbridge Road is flooded, which happens more than you'd think, it can take over an hour. Of course, pedestrians and bikes can get into town in about five minutes using the footbridge."

As the man was leaving, he turned and gave me quite a compliment. "James. I hope you win the bid. You remind me of Jasper Kriss. Good luck."

Susan and I have been working discreetly on our plan. We're almost ready to put forward our bid to the council before the deadline.

The main reason we're keeping things close to our chests is the planning officer, Peter Hogan. Susan's come across him while working with various charities and housing projects. She doesn't want to bring what we're planning to his attention until we're ready. He has a bad reputation. She's heard rumours of him being involved in underhand deals.

Our plan is to refurbish the estate in stages. We'll repair all the houses which have been left to the elements, and goodness knows what else. We propose to pay for council teams to restore the road surfaces.

Susan has spoken to BT and Openreach; they've promised the entire estate can have broadband within six months. We also have plans to complete the unfinished doctors' surgery and the school.

If things go according to plan, we can offer all the houses to people on low incomes.

Over on the business side of the park, there are several commercial buildings that were completed before the council ran out of money. We're hoping to find businesses to move into these units. That way, we can offer employment to local people and bring the entire area back to life.

I've decided on a name for the charity. I'm going to call it MJA Housing Foundation, the initials of my lovely wife and two kids.

It's an ambitious project, but so far, everything seems to be going according to plan.

CHAPTER FIFTY-EIGHT

JAMES

Monday 14th November 2016

It's funny how quickly you can adapt to new things. Four weeks ago, I was penniless and living on the streets. Now I'm like my old self. Not having to worry about money, my confidence has returned, and I walk with my head high instead of looking at people's footwear.

Most days, around lunchtime, I like to go for a walk to clear my head. While I'm out and about, I notice people sitting in doorways asking for change.

I recognise most of them, although a few are new faces. I started out handing each of them a twenty-pound note. But now, if I know they'll spend the money on booze or drugs, I only give them five, and I'll give ten to people trying to help themselves move forward.

Occasionally, I'll buy someone a sandwich or a McDonald's Meal Deal. If they're selling the *Big Issue*, I give them a ten-pound note, take a copy, and tell them to keep the change.

Little Tony is a man of around twenty who's been on the streets for about two years. He's called Little Tony because he's exactly five feet tall and looks like ex-Prime Minister Tony Blair.

His real name's Donald Much. He's very thin and always wears a brightly coloured hat. He tries his hardest to improve his life, but from time to time, he'll revert to taking drugs. Such a shame, as he's highly intelligent.

I stop to chat with him. "Hey, Tony. How are things?"

"Hi, man. Could you spare some change?"

I give him a fiver.

"Yeah. I'm good. Ain't you the guy that used to hang around with Stevie?"

"Yes. But he went back home to look after his mum."

"I saw him yesterday."

"Are you sure?"

"Yeah. Spoke to him and everything. He said he'd moved back. I think his mum's okay now."

"Thanks, Tony."

"No problem, mate."

I give him another five pounds.

I wonder if Stevie's taken over our bedsit at the rear of the Albion. He's the only other person who knows about it, and I know George will look after him if he's there.

I walk around to Shaw Street and go through the front entrance, looking to see if George is around. Behind the reception desk is a woman I've never seen before. She doesn't look very tall and wears her hair neatly tied back. The name tag on her smart freshly-pressed uniform shows me her name's Diane, and she's the assistant manager.

"Hello. Is it possible to speak with George Leeman please? My name is James Sheldon."

She lifts the telephone and dials a number.

"Hello, George. There's a gentleman in reception asking for you. James Sheldon. Okay, I'll let him know. Bye."

She smiles. "George will be with you in a minute. If you'd care to take a seat and wait over there." She points across the entranceway to the comfortable-looking seats on the other side.

I smile back. "Thank you."

Within a minute, George appears and walks over to where I'm seated. His extended hand precedes him, ready to shake mine as he flashes a big smile.

"Hello, Mr Sheldon. It's nice to see you. What brings you back to the Albion?"

"Hello, George. I was wondering if Stevie, the Welsh lad, is occupying the suite out the back."

"As a matter of fact he is. He arrived last night, but I'm not sure he's there now. You'll most likely catch him this evening, or I can pass on a message for you."

"Yes, if you could ask him to pop round and see me at this address?" I hand George one of my newly printed business cards.

"I heard you're starting a charity. It's nice to see someone putting something back into society instead of all the greed, unlike this place. We heard last week they're going to sell the site to a developer. We'll all be out of our jobs in a few weeks."

I gasp. "You're joking. That's terrible. Has the deal gone through yet, do you know?"

"I don't think so, but it won't take long. Mr Atkins, the general manager, was most upset. He would know. Do you want me to ask him?"

"Yes please, George."

He goes over to reception and speaks to Diane, and I see her pick up the phone and talk to someone.

George comes back. "He knows who you are. I told him all about your generosity when you gave me the money. He's going to come out and have a chat – that is, if you've got the time?"

"Yes, George. Not a problem. Let's hear what he has to say."

In my days of enjoying the Albion's amenities, I never encountered the general manager.

A worried-looking man in his early fifties appears. "Hello, I'm Jonathan Atkins. George told me what you've done for him and young Freddie. I'm very pleased to meet you."

"Hello, Jonathan. George tells me the hotel is for sale – do you know if it's actually been sold yet?"

"No. As far as I'm aware, the deal's due to be signed at the end of next week."

"Can I ask you one question? As it currently stands, is the hotel making money? Is it profitable?"

"Actually, it is. It doesn't make a fortune, but it's definitely in the black, and with some investment, it could make a lot more. But the owners have decided to sell it for redevelopment."

"In that case, I only have two more questions. One... would you be happy for me to buy it and keep it running as a hotel? And two... if so, who do I need to speak to?"

George and Jonathan stand in silence, taking in what they've just heard.

Then Jonathan speaks. "I think I can say, on behalf of all the staff, that we would love to have you as the new owner. They're going to shut down the hotel and turn the place into luxury apartments. We'd all lose our jobs, and none of us wants that. It's such a nice place to work.

"To answer your second question, you'll need to speak to Coverdale's Estate Agents who are handling the deal. Ask for Mr Robert Coverdale."

"You mean the place on Albany Street? I'll go over there now and see if he's available."

CHAPTER FIFTY-NINE

JAMES

"Hello, would it be possible to speak with Mr Coverdale please?"

"Do you have an appointment?" asks the smartly dressed, stunning blonde from behind her reception desk.

"No, I don't, but I'm here to see him about the Albion Hotel. It's rather urgent."

"Please, take a seat. I'll see if he's available."

I don't have to wait long. The receptionist walks around from behind the large desk.

"Mr Sheldon, if you'd like to follow me, Mr Coverdale says he can spare you a few minutes."

I follow her to a row of glass-fronted offices stretching across the rear of the ground floor. *Blondie* knocks on the door, opens it and announces me. She stands to one side of the doorway as I squeeze past her and catch the fragrance she is wearing.

"Thank you, Julia," says Mr Coverdale.

She smiles and closes the door.

I stretch out a hand which the man shakes. "Hello, Mr

Coverdale. It's good of you to see me at short notice and without an appointment."

"I do have a few minutes. Julia said you mentioned the Albion Hotel."

"Yes. I understand the sale is at an advanced stage. However I wonder if the owners might be open to a higher offer?"

I notice a grin spread across the estate agent's face.

"I see. As you say, things are close to completion, and the price is rather steep. It's a prime site."

"Yes, I understand – could you indulge me and tell me the price?"

"It would be rather unethical to reveal that to you," he states. After a few seconds though, he adds, "Let's just say somewhere between seventeen and nineteen million pounds. Would that give you an idea?"

"Yes, it would. What if I said I'm prepared to offer twenty million? Oh, and I'm a cash buyer."

Robert Coverdale's expression remains deadpan. It's as if someone telling him they have this amount of cash available is an everyday event. Perhaps in his world, it is!

"If you're serious, I can make a call to my clients. No disrespect, but I would need proof such funds are available."

"I can give you the name of the person at Lloyds Bank who deals with my account: Nigel Prentis."

"Oh yes, I know Nigel. We play golf together. As a matter of fact, I've got a game with him this afternoon. In that case, Mr Sheldon, I see no reason not to put your offer to my clients. Obviously, the other party may come back with a better offer. Would you be prepared to increase yours if that were the case?"

"Let's wait and see what happens, but I am serious. Here's my card."

"This has been a pleasant surprise, Mr Sheldon. I'm sure my clients will let me know shortly, then I'll be in touch. Can I ask why you want to buy the Albion? Are you planning to redevelop it?"

"You may have heard about a homeless man winning one hundred and sixty-eight million pounds on the Lotto. That was me. When I was homeless, I slept behind the hotel. The night porter looked after me, and a couple of the staff were extremely kind. I hate the thought of all those people losing their jobs, so I'm buying the hotel and will continue to run it as it is.

"The hotel manager tells me it makes money. He says that with some refurbishment and modernisation, it could be a good investment. More importantly, it will secure a lot of jobs that would otherwise be lost."

"It's a lovely hotel, and it could be even better. The only reason for the sale is because of a family squabble between the shareholders, so I hope it turns out in your favour."

"Thank you, Mr Coverdale. It was good to meet you, and I look forward to hearing from you."

I walk out of the office and across towards the front door. As I do, I notice the receptionist looking my way. "Thank you, Julia. Have a lovely afternoon," I say then give a big smile.

She smiles back.

I know Miriam would want me to get on with my life, but, as attractive as this woman is, I don't think I'm ready. I'm not sure I ever will be. Miriam, Jack and Abi fill my thoughts every day. Somehow, it wouldn't feel right, as if I were being unfaithful.

As I walk out, I try to put any thoughts of the lovely Julia out of my mind.

The following day, I receive a phone call from Robert Coverdale.

"Good morning, Mr Sheldon. I've spoken with my clients, and they, in turn, have spoken to the other party. My clients have confirmed they would be prepared to accept a bid of twenty-one million. And the other party have said they would step aside at that level."

"Based on what you've told me, I'm prepared to increase my offer."

"I think you've got a good deal. With some extra investment to update the hotel, you could see a very handsome return."

"To be honest, Mr Coverdale, it's more to do with saving the jobs of those who helped me when I needed it. As long as it doesn't lose money, I'm not bothered. Otherwise, the money will sit in a bank somewhere and not do anything worthwhile. This way, the people at the Albion benefit."

After arranging the finer details with Mr Coverdale, I find the phone number for the Albion Hotel and ask to speak with Jonathan Atkins.

"Hello, Mr Atkins? It's James Sheldon. We met yesterday when I came to see George. I wanted you to know, and perhaps you can tell the staff, I expect to be the new owner in the near future.

"My plans will ensure no jobs are lost, and, in fact, I intend to invest in and refurbish all parts of the hotel. I trust you'll stay on to help and advise me. I don't intend to interfere with the running of things."

"Mr Sheldon, I can't tell you how relieved I am to hear this. I, and many of the staff, have been extremely upset by what's happening. With your permission, I'll organise a staff meeting and tell everyone. Thank you so much.

"I know you won't regret the decision. We all want to make a go of it. The staff are a good bunch of people, and they work hard. I'm sure they'll appreciate what you're offering to do."

CHAPTER SIXTY

DAVE

Monday 14th November 2016

Peter Hogan, head of the planning department, is a worried man. He's received a call from a surveyor friend. He explains that he was recently hired to visit Asbury Park, along with two contractors, to write a report on the cost of updating the estate's properties. The man says the people behind it are a new local charity. He tells Peter they are thinking about putting in a bid for the estate.

Peter thanks his friend for the information and places a call to Dave Rex.

"Hi, Dave. I've heard a rumour someone else is thinking of submitting a bid for Asbury Park."

Dave erupts. "Yaaarh! Then put a spanner in its works! Come on, you owe me big time. Get moving and spike it!"

"Yeah. Okay, Dave. I'll do my best."

"Who's behind the bid?"

"It's a woman by the name of Susan Hartman. She's friendly with one or two people on the planning committee.

I've dropped a hint that your bid's around thirty million. I've made sure word will get back to her, so it should put these other people off. There's no way they're going to bid that high."

"Who's this Susan Hartman? I've never heard of her."

"Yeah, I've come across her a few times. A real socialist lefty, you know the type. She's connected with a couple of local social-housing organisations. Now she's working with some rich guy called James Sheldon."

"Sheldon!"

Dave is gripped with rage. He flings the phone across the room before he rushes downstairs. He jumps into his car and drives to the Premier Inn on Etruria Road. The fact the hotel doesn't have a car park does nothing to diminish his mood. Especially when the nearest vacant parking space is two streets away.

Arriving at the hotel reception, Dave asks for James Sheldon's room.

"I'm sorry, but Mr Sheldon has left the hotel."

"Then I'll bloody well wait here until he gets back."

The aggression in his voice takes the young lady by surprise. She makes a noise as if her throat tightens, but she manages to reply.

"No, I'm sorry, sir. I mean he's not staying with us anymore. He's checked out."

Dave slams his fist down on the reception desk and shouts an expletive before hurtling out, leaving the girl trembling.

He walks back to his car, unsure of what to do to catch

up with the man who stole his ticket. Where does he start? He gets into his Mercedes and drives off at speed. He decides to head for the gym to let off some steam.

The car in front of him stops without warning, and he bumps into the back of it. He gets out and sees there isn't much damage, especially to his car. He walks forward to the driver's door, ready to have a go at the idiot who, in his opinion, is at fault for stopping so quickly. Upon reaching the other vehicle, he discovers it's a female driver.

"Bloody typical, you stupid bitch. You shouldn't be allowed on the road."

"Don't speak to me like that," she says, stepping out of her car.

When she utters words about exchanging insurance details, Dave sees red and hits her squarely in the face with a full punch. As she lies on the ground, he kicks her in the face. The sight of blood pouring from her nose only seems to get him more worked up. One final kick to the head before he gets into his car and drives off, smiling. She certainly won't stop suddenly again.

Pumped up from the altercation, he drives off towards the gym. He'll follow it up by getting a relaxing massage. He hopes it will help lower his blood pressure. The doctor told him it was on the high side during his last medical exam.

The gym is part of a leisure complex on a modern business park. It's less than five minutes from the hotel. The location means there's room for a wide range of facilities. These include tennis, badminton, squash courts, and indoor and outdoor swimming pools.

It's one thirty p.m., and Dave is heading for the gym's first-floor café bar. He finds a table by the front window. It overlooks the other buildings across the business park.

He watches as a vast range of cars and vans come and go from the wholesale cash-and-carry warehouse. As he stares out the window, his mind returns to the fateful day he visited the convenience store.

He wasn't even meant to be in the centre of town. He was only there because the present he had ordered for his mother's birthday hadn't arrived on time. If only he'd been more careful and checked his ticket after bumping into the tramp.

Dave's line of thought is broken by the waitress asking if he is ready to order.

After finishing his meal, he leaves the gym complex. He decides to make a tour of his three legitimate businesses.

With everything running smoothly, he returns home. He'll think about it overnight, but he might consider increasing his bid for Asbury Park. He puts the thought out of his mind.

He needs a drink and goes in search of his unopened bottle of Jack Daniel's.

The rest of his day will be a blur.

CHAPTER SIXTY-ONE

JAMES

Tuesday 15th November 2016

Lunchtime arrives, but there's still no sign of Stevie. Is it possible that George and Little Tony forgot to pass on my message? Stevie's my best mate, and I want to share my good fortune with him; he's the reason I'm still alive.

I walk down West Street and up towards Market Square, passing the store where I bought my winning ticket. It just goes to show, one small decision can change your entire life.

As I approach the market, I can see Little Tony. He's talking to Young Ned, who has his dog, Buddy, with him. I go over and say hello. Young Ned looks at me in a strange way. People dressed like me don't normally go up and chat.

"Sorry to bother you," I say. "Have either of you seen Stevie from Rhyl?"

Tony's first response is: "You couldn't spare any change, could you?"

I give them a fiver each. I don't receive any thanks but I don't expect to.

Young Ned chirps up. "I saw him about an hour back. He was over at Kirby's."

I thank him for the info and see they're both already leaving. I guess they're heading for the nearest off-licence.

I walk back to the West Street office and grab my bike from the rack at the rear of the building. Five minutes later, I reach my destination, but don't see Stevie.

I rest my bike against the wall near the two benches where the group I'm looking for are sitting and standing around. Most of them have cans of beer in their hands.

"Hi, has anyone seen Stevie from Rhyl?" I enquire.

"He's gone to the offy," I'm informed by one of the guys standing near the benches. I don't recognise him. "He'll be back soon," he slurs.

I turn round and look across to the opposite side of the road. About a hundred yards down is the small shop run by Mr and Mrs Miah. Years ago, it was also a post office, but Royal Mail closed it down. All that's left of that side of the business is the bright-red post box outside. Letter collections are once a day at five thirty p.m., but there's nowhere to buy a stamp.

As I look over, I see Stevie coming out of the shop. He stops and opens his can of beer then staggers back in my direction. As he approaches, I can see he's a little worse for drink. He hasn't seen me since the Lotto win. He looks the same, but I must look a lot different.

"Hi, Stevie. It's me, James."

It takes a few seconds for him to register, staring at me while leaning forward. Finally, he realises who I am.

"Hey, James," he cries, rushing forward to give me a hug while keeping his can in his right hand.

I'm happy to see him and hug him back, even at the risk

of his beer spilling all over my nice new clothes. This is my best buddy.

"Didn't you get my messages from Little Tony and George yesterday?"

"Yeah, I did, but I wasn't sure what to do. I read the newspapers – you're a big shot now. I didn't think you'd want me around."

"Stevie, that's so wrong. Without you, I wouldn't be here. The money doesn't change a thing. You're my best friend. We've been through a lot, and I wouldn't have made it on my own. Mates stick together. My good fortune means I can repay my debt and help a friend. You're someone I trust. Someone to help with the big plans I've got. I really need you, mate."

He seems shocked. But, even in his current state, I can see the sincerity of my words and the passion in my voice getting across to him. Even I'm choking up a little.

"I've rented a two-bedroom apartment while I'm waiting for a house purchase to go through. I want you to move in with me. I need your help and advice with the housing charity I'm setting up."

"You don't need me in your place, cramping your style with the ladies."

"There've been no ladies in my life since my wife, and there's not likely to be. This could be a good thing for both of us. How about we work side by side? We could help a lot of people off the streets and give a lot of couples a decent place to start a family. Think what we can achieve together – what do you say?"

"Okay, matey. A nice warm bed would be good. I'll need to collect my things from the Albion. George said he'd keep an eye on them."

"Yeah, George is great. Let's go grab your stuff, and I'll take you to our new place."

I use my mobile to call a taxi. While we're waiting, I take my bike across the road and lock it to the metal bike rack in front of Barclays Bank. I'll come back and collect it later today or tomorrow.

CHAPTER SIXTY-TWO

JAMES

Three minutes later, our taxi arrives. The driver says cans of beer aren't allowed in the cab, so Stevie gives his to one of the other people hanging around. We both get in and head for the Albion.

Then I give the driver the address: the Meadowcroft on Keele Street. It's a small complex of seven apartments close to the railway station, set over four floors, two flats per level, with the penthouse occupying the entire top floor.

I pay the driver, and Stevie and I take the stairs to Flat 3. We walk into the spacious lounge. On the far side are floor-to-ceiling windows with beech-colour frames. A door leads out to a balcony large enough for a table with four chairs and a dome-topped BBQ in the corner.

The lounge area has a long black leather sofa. It curves around ninety degrees and can seat six people. In front of it stands a black coffee table. There's also a maple-wood table complete with four high-back leather dining chairs. The TV is on a black glass stand that sits adjacent to the windows.

Between that and the dining table is a black wall unit. It

contains books and ornaments left behind by the previous tenant. The kitchen can best be described as compact, with a partition wall between it and the lounge area.

At the front of the apartment are two good-sized bedrooms. Mine has a king-size bed. Stevie's has a double. Each bedroom has a large closet with floor-to-ceiling sliding doors for clothes. And each has its own en suite bathroom.

The apartment comes furnished right down to the kettle and built-in microwave. These are the items that get the most use out of everything in the apartment.

I show Stevie his room.

"Okay, here we are. I can see you don't have much in the way of clothes. We can go into town in the next couple of days and find you a few things."

"I don't want to be any trouble," he says in a more sober voice than earlier.

"Stevie, let's get things straight. I've had some good luck, and I'd like to share some of it with my best mate in the whole world. If it were the other way around, I have no doubt you'd look after me."

"So, who's this 'best mate in the whole world' you mentioned?" he asks with a grin.

I know I've got the Stevie I love back. Along with his sense of humour.

"It's you, you muppet," I say, leaving him in no doubt.

We give each other a big man-hug. No can of beer to get in the way this time.

"Tell you what," he says, "now I've sobered up, I'm feeling a bit peckish. Is there any food in the place?"

"You must be joking. I can't cook to save my life. There's plenty of restaurants across the road. Let's go and see what you fancy."

I put on the thick coat I purchased a couple of days ago. The nights are starting to get colder – and Stevie puts on a coat from the bag he collected from the Albion. It's seen better days, and I make a note to buy him a new one, but for now, food is our main concern.

We walk across to Clarendon Square, with its large selection of restaurants. Stevie likes the look of Nando's, so we opt for that. It will give me a chance to explain my plans for transforming Asbury Park to him.

An hour and a quarter later, we walk back to the apartment, still chatting away. He's full of great suggestions.

CHAPTER SIXTY-THREE

JAMES

Tuesday, 15th November 2016

Yesterday, Susan and I had a meeting. She suggested we should employ someone to handle the PR side of things. She feels it will demonstrate to the council and the local media that we're serious about Asbury Park.

She explained that a lot of the work we're planning to do needs to be capable of impressing the kind of influential people who could help us in the future. Apparently, it's what all the leading charities do. And it could open a lot of doors that otherwise would remain closed.

So she put details on Facebook and LinkedIn. Within an hour we had five people apply. Susan has said she'll leave the applications open until tomorrow morning and run the interviews in the afternoon and Thursday morning.

Peter Hogan puts through a call to Dave Rex.

"Dave, I've just seen the charity Susan Hartman runs is looking for a public relations manager."

Dave's retort is gruff. "Yeah, Peter. And this affects me how?"

"Well, my niece Alison Crook works in PR. She's between jobs right now. I thought, if she applied and got the job, she could feed us inside information."

Dave's tone lightens. "Hmmm. Good thinking. I tell you what… I'll sweeten the pot for your niece. Tell her if she gets the job, I'll give her ten grand in cash. Plus a further ten grand if she can pull off something to stop them winning the bid."

"That's extremely generous, Dave. I'll call her now and ask her to apply."

Friday 18th November 2016

Susan Hartman is reviewing the CVs of the nine PR manager candidates. She's narrowed it down to two. Her first choice is Felicity, but she needs to give a month's notice to her current employers.

There's a knock at the office door. "Hello, Miss Hartman. Remember me? Alison Crook. You interviewed me on Wednesday afternoon for the position of PR manager. I was passing by, and I thought I'd pop in and ask if you had any further questions. And to let you know I can start on Monday if that would help?"

Susan is impressed. Here is someone who seems like a go-getter. This girl is clearly very keen. Exactly the sort of person the charity needs. It seems fate has stepped in and given Susan an easy choice.

After a brief chat, Susan announces, "Alison, we look forward to seeing you at nine o'clock on Monday."

"You mean I've got the job? Thank you, you won't regret it."

Alison walks along West Street to Starbucks. She orders an Americano and a blueberry muffin, finds an empty table at the back and sits down. She pulls out her phone.

"Hello, Uncle Peter. I got the job at the charity. I start on Monday. What do you need me to do?"

Tuesday 22nd November 2016

Dave has invited Alison to meet him at his apartment, along with her uncle. The three of them are sitting in Dave's lounge.

"Your uncle Peter has told me a lot of good things about you, and well done for getting the job at the charity. Having someone on the inside and a way to know what they're planning is going to help.

"I'm not sure what your uncle's told you, but the guy behind the charity stole my Lotto ticket. Now he's trying to buy the Asbury Park estate. I need you to find a way to stop him from winning the bid.

"Your uncle is trying to ensure his fellow planning committee members vote in favour of my bid. They have the final say on who wins. So the more I can discredit this James Sheldon character, the better. It will help my chances of getting the council to drop him.

"I've already tried other methods, but it's complicated. I

need a way to let people know this guy stole my ticket, so I can reclaim my money – or what's left of it.

"Oh, and while I think of it, let's get the money out of the way, shall we? As promised, here's ten thousand in cash. And you'll get another ten when the job's done."

Alison Crook listens intently before speaking. "I've come up with a few ideas. I think the best way to start is with a negative publicity campaign. To show people this is someone who can't be trusted.

"The council's public image is everything to them. They need the public to believe they have high moral standards. That's the thing they'll try to maintain at all costs. Local elections are coming up shortly. I'd imagine they're not unduly concerned about who wins the Asbury Park bid, as long as they come out of it looking good. After all, it doesn't affect them.

"They can put the word out they've sold the site to the best bidder in the long-term interest of the town. All they're concerned about is keeping their seats on the council.

"It won't be revealed to the public if there's a higher bid. It's all done behind closed doors. And even if word does get out that they've accepted the lower of two bids, it'll all be forgotten in a few days.

"I don't know if you recall. A couple of years ago there was that bus shelter which cost thirty thousand pounds, despite not a single bus actually stopping there. That was front-page news for a couple of days, but it's long forgotten.

"I've seen it with the PR work I've done in the past. Once they've been re-elected, all they're interested in are the benefits. The official dinners, the trips to overseas twinned towns, the fact-finding tours to hot places with all expenses paid, and so on."

Peter Hogan steps in. "What Alison's saying is true. As long as the publicity doesn't affect them, it doesn't matter. In the chambers of the council, it's understood you stick together, even if you know one or two of your colleagues have an agenda, because they're aware of your own past. Everyone covers for everyone else."

Alison nods in agreement.

Wednesday 23rd November 2016

After leaving work at the MJA offices, Alison Crook drives to Dave Rex's apartment.

They sit at the desk in his home office.

Alison passes across two sheets of neatly typed paper.

"Since we spoke yesterday, I've given this a lot of thought. I've prepared a press release. Please have a look and tell me what you think. The best way to do this is for me to leak it to a couple of my contacts in the local media. It will put doubt in the minds of the council, and make people think this guy, James Sheldon, is untrustworthy. It should also paint you as the hero."

Dave reads the entire document, and a smile spreads across his face. "It's bloody perfect."

"In that case," says Alison, "all you need to do is let me know when you're ready, and I'll send it out."

CHAPTER SIXTY-FOUR

GERRY PAYNE

Wednesday 23rd November 2016

It's six in the evening, and Gerry Payne is relaxing with a half-pint of lager. He's reflecting on the decision he made nine months ago to retire from the police force. Now he wishes he'd done it a lot sooner!

This time last year, he'd still have been over an hour away from leaving work if he was lucky. Instead, he and his wife, Paddy, are the proud owners of the Fenton Motel on the edge of Trentbridge.

At first, they considered changing the name. In the end, they decided the sensible thing was to keep the name on which its reputation had been built.

What's more, the past few months have given Gerry plenty of opportunities to use his detective skills. He pretty much knows which couples are married, and which ones might well be married – but not to each other.

When he is serving at the bar, he can work out which couples are meeting up because they're in love, and which are here to avoid being seen by anyone who knows them. It keeps him amused. Once a detective, always a detective!

And the change has done wonders for his blood pressure, not to mention the more sociable working hours.

To update the place, he and Paddy are currently spending forty thousand pounds refurbishing the bedrooms. The work is being carried out gradually so they can keep the motel open, so as not to lose goodwill and customers.

Since taking over the business, one of the things that has caught Gerry's eye are the four dodgy-looking men. They meet up in the coffee bar lounge every two weeks.

What first came to his mind was that the times they meet seemed to vary rather than always occur on the same day and time. He knows this is a trait of those not wanting to be noticed by other people.

On one occasion, he was at the rear of the hotel, discussing extending the living quarters with a builder. He saw two of these men exchange something from the boots of their cars. But what really made him suspicious was when one of them spilt hot black coffee on himself, and let out a few words in Russian. His partner laughed and said something in the same language.

Gerry's many years of experience told him this had all the markings of a drug deal. That, and the fact he is certain he recognised a face he last saw around eight years ago on a case he was working with the local drug squad.

Gerry recalls that the guy was a small-time dealer. It could be he's moved up the ladder over the years? On the last occasion, the four men came into the coffee lounge, and he was finally able to recall the guy's name: Dave Rex.

As they left, Gerry managed to take photos of the four men without being spotted.

At first, he thought about reporting the details to Diana Wakefield. She had secured a promotion from detective inspector to the role of DCI.

But she isn't available when he calls, so Gerry reports his suspicions to DCI Andy Stone. He gives him the car registration numbers and forwards copies of the photos via *WhatsApp*.

He knows, from the pattern he has observed, roughly when their meetings will take place. They alternate between a Tuesday one time and a Wednesday the next. The times vary between ten a.m. and four p.m. From this, Gerry has worked out that their next meeting will be on Tuesday the sixth of December.

Andy asks Gerry if they can put an undercover female police officer at the motel to work as a waitress.

Gerry agrees on the condition that any arrests will be made away from the motel. He wants to preserve its good reputation.

CHAPTER SIXTY-FIVE

JAMES

Monday 28th November 2016

It's been a busy morning dealing with all the last-minute paperwork. We're double-checking everything so we can put in our bid for Asbury Park.

Susan has been talking to her contacts in the council, and it appears that, so far, there's only one other bid. It's from an organisation called DR Social Housing Ltd and, they've heard, it's for thirty million – much higher than we expected.

We've decided not to submit our bid until the very last moment because Susan has been warned by two of her friends within the council that the head of the planning department, Peter Hogan, might be involved with the other bidder. They've said he's not a man to be trusted and that he might try to find a way to sabotage our bid.

Wednesday 30th November 2016

Today was the last day for submitting bids. We delivered

ours just ten minutes before the noon deadline in a wax-sealed envelope.

I've taken photos of the envelope, so we can check whether someone's tried to tamper with it, and sent them to Susan's contact. He'll be at the meeting when the council open the bids and will know if it's been opened. I realise it sounds a little over the top, but, as a former detective, I know how devious some people can be. And we can't afford to take any chances.

Now all we can do is wait and see what happens.

The bids will be opened at a closed-door council meeting on the 1st of December. The final announcements to the press and public won't take place for a further two weeks. But Susan's contact will tell us – *off the record* – if we've been successful.

In the hope ours is the winning bid, we've been hard at work. We now have the costs for the rebuilding of the bridge and road infrastructure, likely to be in the region of forty million. It's no wonder other developers have turned down the opportunity to buy Asbury Park in the past.

So all we can do is hope and pray.

CHAPTER SIXTY-SIX

PETER

Thursday 1st December 2016

Peter Hogan is sitting in the council chamber alongside the other committee members and the council's legal team.

Yesterday was the closing deadline for bids on the various plots of land the council are selling off. They are reviewing the bids ahead of their final decision, which will be made in two weeks. It seems most of the lots have attracted a good number of bids. The council hopes to reach their thirty million target to cover the budget deficit.

So far, the winning bids have produced a total of twenty-one million.

Now they have come to Asbury Park, the final lot. It has only attracted two bids.

The clerk opens the first envelope. He looks at the contents and addresses the other members, "Ladies and gentlemen, the first bid for the Asbury Park estate is from DR Social Housing. Their bid is for fourteen million pounds."

Peter Hogan smiles: without telling him, Dave Rex had decided to raise his bid. Hopefully, it will make him the clear winner. With a guide price of ten million, it's unlikely anybody will offer more than that.

The clerk turns to the second envelope, still sealed with red wax. He slits along the edge with his letter opener.

The council members are silent as they watch the clerk read the contents. Finally, he looks up. His face gives nothing away. "The second bid is from an organisation called MJA Housing Foundation. Their bid is for" – he looks around the room to see he has everyone's attention, then carefully enunciates every next word – "thirty-five million, two hundred and eighty-eight thousand pounds."

There are eruptions of laughter and hoots. One member conveys his delight by banging his fists on the table. Peter Hogan manages to cover his anger with a veiled smile.

An hour later, Peter goes down to the basement car park. He sits in his car, almost in tears thinking about the quarter of a million that has slipped from his fingers. How will he explain it to Monique? But right now, he must give the news to Dave Rex.

Peter dials his number and starts to explain, but quickly has to pull the phone away from his head before Dave's torrent of abuse bursts his eardrum. The phone goes dead. Peter is glad he called Dave instead of telling him face to face.

He's still sitting in his car two minutes later, wondering what to do when Dave calls back; this time he's much calmer.

"Listen, Peter, you screwed up, big time. Redeem yourself and the quarter of a million can still be yours. I want Alison to send out the press release today. Tell her to follow it up with a publicity campaign. I want her to make it so bad the council won't touch that bastard with a fucking barge-pole. Then I need you to make sure all the committee members back my bid, even if it is lower."

Peter returns to his office. The situation is not looking good, but he's confident he can still turn things around. He should be feeling depressed. Luckily, there's one thing stopping him. Monique, the twenty-six-year-old goddess who makes his life worth living.

He's planning to see her tonight but will put off telling her about the money problem for now. He's more interested in what she'll be wearing. She once answered the door naked, but he told her he prefers it when she dresses up.

He particularly likes it when she wears her secretary outfit. He relishes slowly undoing the buttons of her blouse. It's not something he'd enjoy doing with his own secretary, Cynthia. She's fifty-four and looks like the character from the movie *Mrs Doubtfire*, only more rounded.

CHAPTER SIXTY-SEVEN

JAMES

Thursday 1st December 2016

Susan has just received a phone call from her main contact at the council. He told her there were only two bids on the table for Asbury Park, and ours was by far the highest. He wouldn't tell Susan how much the other bid was for, or who placed it. He explained he wouldn't be comfortable giving out information that pertained to other people.

So everything seems to be going well for us. Stoneman's, the lawyers, have confirmed the Charity Commission have approved our application.

My offer to buy the Albion Hotel is a couple of days away from completion. Once the contract is signed, I plan to bring in a specialist hotel refurbishment company. I'll insist they keep the character of the hotel, but update the décor and improve any outdated facilities.

From our initial talks, the budget should be in the region of three million. I'm amazed how quickly I've come to accept such large amounts of money as if they were normal. I guess now they are!

Stevie's working in the office and proving to be a human dynamo. What's more, Susan's taken to him, and the pair work well together. It pleases me to see them both getting on and being so committed to the project.

Yes, fingers crossed, everything's working out far better than we expected.

CHAPTER SIXTY-EIGHT

ALISON CROOK

Friday 2nd December 2016

Yesterday afternoon, Alison received a frantic phone call from her uncle Peter. In response, she immediately sent the press release to the local newspaper. They published it as today's front-page story.

'Homeless Man Stole My Lotto Ticket and Charity Idea.'

The contents are spread across pages four and five. Having seen the impact it has made, Alison decides to send copies out to the national press:

> A well-respected local businessman has come forward after he discovered his winning Lotto ticket had been stolen. This is alongside his plans to help the local community.
>
> In his report to the police, local entrepreneur David Rex says he was about to go on a two-week business trip to Spain. He popped into Tindall's in

Market Street to buy some wrapping paper. While he was there, he also purchased a Lotto ticket using a regular set of numbers.

He goes on to say that as he left the store, he was tripped up, leaving him dazed and confused. Subsequently, he discovered his Lotto ticket and a file were missing. It contained plans of his bid for the redevelopment of the Asbury Park estate.

He didn't notice the file was missing until his return. It was then he read the story about the homeless man winning the Lotto. He recognised his photo in the newspaper as the man who had assaulted him at the store.

He has since discovered the same individual is behind a rival bid for the Asbury Park estate.

Mr Rex says hard work has been the key to building up his business empire over the past ten years. He currently employs over thirty people. He states the development of the social housing is his way of giving back to the local community.

He says he believes the rival plans for Asbury Park are a smokescreen. He thinks the real idea is to transform the estate into a private development. Creating a "millionaires' row" of large houses. None of which will provide any benefit for ordinary people.

When asked to provide proof, Mr Rex says his bid to the council had been discussed with council officials before his business trip.

A statement from Local Planning Committee Chairman Peter Hogan confirms this. He states he can bear out the facts presented by David Rex.

He says, "Mr Rex came up with the idea to refurbish and repair the eight hundred and eighty houses on the estate. He wants to offer them to local families at rents far below those being charged by private landlords. I think this is a magnificent gesture.

"Mr Rex is a well-respected figure in our community. I would not like to see such plans upset by someone with ulterior motives. What he proposes will give struggling families a chance to build a future. They will be able to bring up their children in nice houses with their own gardens. The council totally supports the project."

Mr Rex also confirms that he has taken legal advice. He is currently in the process of issuing proceedings. He states he has overwhelming evidence he's the owner of the winning ticket, including a witness. He is confident the courts will agree.

His lawyer has commented that it is only a matter of time before the case goes to court. He then fully expects his client to be able to claim the Lotto winnings.

Mr Rex is quoted as saying, "This project includes plans for a doctors' surgery and school. It could benefit many hundreds of people in our community. I would hate to see Asbury Park being turned into a gated community for a few wealthy individuals. My legal team and I are working around the clock to ensure this doesn't happen."

Dave Rex is sitting at the desk in his home office with a

copy of the newspaper spread open across the surface. He reads every word again and again. It was lucky Alison was able to pass on her inside information about Sheldon's plans for the estate.

Dave lifts his engraved cut-glass tumbler of Jack Daniel's. He savours a mouthful of the golden liquid tingling his throat.

He decides it's time to put step two of his plan into motion. He calls Peter Hogan and tells him to start contacting the other planning committee members. It's time to begin stirring things up, persuade them they should look at accepting the alternative. Even if the offer is lower. Remind them that, with this bid, they have already reached their thirty-million-pound target. Tell them he's received phone calls and messages from many highly influential people. He is to say they want nothing to do with James Sheldon or his bid.

Right now, Dave can only hope the council officials are reading their copies of the newspaper. If they are, he hopes they believe James Sheldon *did* steal the ticket.

Dave sits back in his office chair and ponders. It seems like things are now beginning to go his way. He knows if he can destroy Sheldon's reputation, the council will drop him like a red-hot poker.

He knew he was right the day they collided in the convenience store: the man is a 'human piece of crap'. And everyone knows what you do with that stuff. You flush it down the toilet and dispose of it once and for all.

And that's precisely what he's planning to do with James Sheldon.

CHAPTER SIXTY-NINE

JAMES

Friday 2nd December 2016

I'm feeling physically sick. I've read an article in the local newspaper about a man who claims I stole his winning Lotto ticket. He also states I stole his plans to redevelop Asbury Park. It's not true. Why is he saying all this?

And to make matters worse, I've received a registered letter in the post. It's from a lawyer acting on behalf of someone called Dave Rex. I'd never heard of him before today, but there's a photo of him in the newspaper article, and I recognise him as Mr Angry from the convenience store.

I remember the encounter, and now he claims the winning ticket was his. Did it happen that way, or is he trying to trick me into thinking that's what transpired?

I remember the moment my Lotto ticket fell to the floor. Is it possible they got mixed up? Did I pick up the wrong ticket, as he claims? I'm honestly not sure.

According to the letter from his lawyer, if this goes to court, I'll have to return all the winnings. The thought of losing the money isn't what's worrying me. I've never been after riches – you don't join the police to become rich. The whole idea is to give people a decent home at a price that gives them a chance to make something of their lives. It's heartbreaking.

All this worry is not what I had hoped to experience. My head's spinning, and I can feel one of my migraines coming on. I haven't experienced a bad one for a long time.

I'm trying to determine the best course of action. Should I fight the case or save myself the aggravation and expense? I'm not sure what to do.

One of the things I need to do is explain the situation to Susan and Stevie. They're the people who matter to me and have helped me put the entire plan for Asbury Park together. I couldn't have done it without them. And they deserve to know the facts.

Perhaps one option would be to try to form a partnership with Dave Rex to see the project to fruition. Maybe if I give him the money, I can get a written agreement that the project will be completed. Or is it possible he would settle for fifty per cent of the winnings?

Of the hundred and sixty-eight million, I've already given two million to Martin Hammond for the two-pound stake money. And yesterday I transferred twenty-one million for the purchase of the Albion Hotel. All other expenses to date have been covered by the interest received from the savings accounts.

So I still have over one hundred and forty-five million from the original winnings left in the bank. If I offer him seventy million, that will leave me with seventy-five million. That's the amount I intended to invest in Asbury Park and the rebuilding of the bridge.

I'm not a lawyer, but I studied basic law at university, so I know court cases aren't cheap and can take a year or more to get to court. I just hope Dave Rex isn't too greedy. Is it possible he'll think taking a large chunk of the money now, rather than waiting years, would be best?

Perhaps I should consider my options for a couple of days and then make Mr Rex an offer. Yes. Maybe he'll accept an offer, and then things can progress as planned. Of course, after the forty million for the new bridge, surgery and school, this won't leave anything for redeveloping the houses. Or refurbishing the Albion Hotel. But at least the nightmare would be over.

I need to speak with someone who specialises in this kind of thing and get them to test the water by sending an offer to Dave Rex's lawyers. Will it work, or will Mr Rex want it all? If it *was* his ticket, then he's entitled to it.

If it weren't for the Asbury Park project, I'd hand over every penny, but this is so important to me. I remember the tiny first-floor council flat I grew up in. No garden, damp patches on the walls, and the neighbours from hell. I wouldn't wish that on anyone. All those eight hundred and eighty families deserve to have a better future. I can't let everyone down.

Of course, I must remember this is not a man to be trusted. We're talking about the same person who burned a twenty-pound note in front of me when I was homeless.

I recall our fracas at the convenience store. At the time, I had a bad feeling our paths would cross again.

The way things are going, I could lose everything and end up back on the streets.

Even the thought sends a shiver down my spine.

CHAPTER SEVENTY

JAMES

Monday 5th December 2016

I've had the weekend to mull over Friday's correspondence from Dave Rex's lawyers. After much thought, I've decided the best course of action is to seek legal advice. I've done a Google search and made a couple of phone calls. As a result, it seems the best lawyer in town for this type of situation is Clinton Palmer from Palmer and Sands.

I call and speak with Mr Palmer, who, when told of the sums involved, agrees to put aside his arranged lunch meeting.

The offices of Palmer and Sands are in one of the most impressive buildings in Trentbridge. Built less than three years ago, it has an arch-shaped frontage made entirely of tinted glass. It stands on the corner of Drayton Road.

Mr Palmer, the firm's senior partner, has an office on the top floor.

I arrive ten minutes early for the appointment. This doesn't stop him keeping me waiting five minutes past the agreed time. Once I'm ushered into the lawyer's plush office and offered a drink – to which my reply is "Water, please" – I'm invited to sit.

I produce a file with all the correspondence and pass it across the desk. I wait the six minutes it takes the lawyer, costing me eight hundred pounds an hour, to read the letters. Then he looks up and smiles.

"An interesting case," he comments as he leans back in his swivel chair and runs his hand through his hair.

He doesn't ask if there's any truth in the matter of who purchased the Lotto ticket.

"As I see it, you currently hold the best cards. It would be up to the other side to prove beyond reasonable doubt that Mr, er" – he looks down at the paperwork – "that Mr Rex bought the ticket. He states that these were a set of numbers he used every week. However, beyond a single example of a ticket with these numbers on it, he offers no further proof. That one occasion could merely be a coincidence. It doesn't prove anything. Cases like this can take months, even years, to come to court, and then it's down to the judge to decide.

"Mr Rex could, of course, apply for the money to be frozen pending the outcome of the case. I cannot see a court agreeing to that. In my opinion, we write to the other side and inform them we will fight this every step of the way. It's going to be extremely costly for him to proceed. Do you have any indication of his current financial situation?"

"No. I don't know this man at all."

"If you wish, I can have someone check him out for you.

Do you have any idea as to how you would like me to proceed?"

"I've been going over things in my mind. It's true what he says about us bumping into each other at the convenience store that day. But not what he says about me stealing his file or ticket. We both fell to the floor, and I picked up the ticket I thought was mine. He could be telling the truth about it being his. I honestly don't know.

"My main concern is the charity I've set up. We're hoping to buy Asbury Park from the council. The idea is to refurbish the houses and offer them to deserving local families at low rents. We also have plans to add a school and doctors' surgery. In total it will cost around seventy-five million.

"So my thought is to offer this man fifty million right away to settle out of court. However, I'm not sure that will keep him happy, which is why I decided to come and see you."

"If you feel he may have a strong case and you want it to go away, then such an offer would, in my opinion, be hard to resist. Fifty million pounds is more than enough for a good lifestyle. Of course, it all depends on how strongly we word the offer. I can prepare a draft letter and email you a copy for your approval before sending it over to the opposing party. I can mark the offer 'without prejudice' so it cannot be used in court."

As a former police detective, I'm aware of this legal phrase. If the other party rejects the offer, it's as if the offer was never made. In my heart, I think this is the best course of action. I don't think this man's going to go away, and I'd like to see the Asbury Park project get underway without any delays.

"Would you please go ahead and draft the letter. The sooner things are settled, the better, as far as I'm concerned."

"Due to the urgency of the situation, I'm happy to cancel the appointments I have for this afternoon. I'll have the letter emailed over for your approval before three thirty. Then, if you agree with the contents, I can have it sent out today. I'll make it clear the offer of fifty million pounds is non-negotiable. I'll add that they can have the money within forty-eight hours of agreeing to it. Is that going to be a problem?"

I tell him that will be fine.

"That should make them sit up and take notice. If I were working for the other party, I'd be tempted to advise them to accept the offer. Of course, I don't know which way they'll decide to jump. It just so happens that the person acting for the other party is someone I know. It's possible he'll recommend his client accepts your offer, but, of course, there are no guarantees."

I leave the meeting still confused. Now it's down to Dave Rex and his lawyers to decide.

My worry is that the lawyers may think they can make far higher fees by prolonging the case. They could urge their client to take the matter further.

From my days as a police officer, I've seen what some unscrupulous lawyers will do to enhance their income. Some of them are honest, but with a few, I'd always count my fingers after shaking their hand.

The migraine is really starting to kick in. The only way to relieve the pain is to take some strong painkillers and lie down in a dark room with no noise.

I return to my car and somehow manage to drive to the offices on West Street. I have my own private office for times when I need to be alone, and this is definitely one of those occasions. I go over to the only window in the room and pull the blind's cord, to make the room as dark as possible.

I sit in my office chair and place a cushion on the desk. I put my head down to rest, to try to make it stop pounding. I've asked not to be disturbed, and, as this is very unusual, I can sense Susan and Stevie are worried about me. Perhaps they think all this has got to me and I'm feeling depressed.

The project on Asbury Park is my passion. Helping other people comes first; I have little interest in the money: no fancy car, no Rolex watch, and no expensive executive toys. I'm not even interested in women. I just wish my lovely Miriam was still here.

Ouch, the noise. I forgot to turn my mobile to silent. The ring doesn't do anything for my migraine. As I press the answer button, I notice it is three thirty.

"Hello, Mr Sheldon. It's Clinton Palmer. I've just emailed you the draft letter. If you could have a read and let me know whether you'd like any changes made. Otherwise, I can get it into today's post and across to the other side. I'll wait to hear from you, but if you could let me know before four thirty, then it can all be done today."

I thank him for undertaking the work so quickly and promise to check his email straight away, which I do. I find a short note plus an attachment. I click to open the attachment and then print it out on the printer next to my desk. The letter is full of the usual lawyer jargon.

It's exceptionally well written and presents our side of the case vigorously. I just hope it will have the desired effect. I can't see anything which I feel could be improved. I see no reason to make any changes, so I call Mr Palmer, and I'm put through by his secretary.

I tell him I'm happy with the contents of the letter. I send an email confirming my instructions. I then transfer the fifty million pounds into the lawyers' expense account. I send written instructions to allow them to pay the guy who claims he had the winning Lotto ticket – if Mr Rex agrees to drop the court action and abide by the terms laid out in the lawyer's letter.

The migraine seems to be getting worse, and I decide I can't face doing anything more today. I go through to the main office and tell everyone I don't feel very well and I'm going home. Stevie asks if I would like him to drive me home, and I say that would be good.

As we leave the office, I can see everyone looking concerned. They can tell I'm not my usual cheerful self.

Stevie takes my keys and unlocks the car. While he drives, I stretch out across the back seat, trying to rest.

I guess another thing on my mind is seeing all the shops filled with Christmas stuff. It reminds me how much I miss my family.

I'm at the lowest I've been in a long time.

Yesterday, I made a fool of myself. It was my wife's birthday. I saw a woman walking along the street. For a brief moment, I thought I recognised her and rushed over, calling the lady 'Miriam'.

She looked at me as if I was mad. I haven't told anyone, but I'm feeling extremely depressed on top of everything else.

Dealing with the present is hard enough. The past? That's a whole other ballgame.

CHAPTER SEVENTY-ONE

DAVE

Monday 5th December 2016

Dave Rex is having a good day. Everything finally seems to be going his way.

The publicity campaign against James Sheldon is gaining momentum; Alison has been in contact with the local TV station, and the national media is beginning to take an interest. She thinks it should help the council come over to his side.

And that's not the only good news he's received.

Dave's drugs business is booming. In fact, he is meeting the two Russians tomorrow for the biggest deal they have done so far. His order for this fortnightly meeting is forty thousand pounds' worth of cocaine. And his escort business is also on the increase. The profits keep rolling in.

There's only one final thing that will make his day. Dealing with the 'human piece of crap' who stole his winning ticket.

Now he's ready to put his plan into action. It's time to

dispose of James Sheldon and get his hands on the Lotto money. All he needs to do is make some calls to double-check everything is in place for tomorrow.

His first call is to one of the porters at the Grand Hotel. Dave has been paying him at least two hundred pounds a week to find clients for his escorts. It's mainly businessmen staying in the area for a night or two who want some female company.

For the porter, it's easy money: a few phone calls and once a week he gets a brown envelope with a cash payment. Today, Dave is calling to confirm he has followed the instructions he's been given to the letter.

All the porter has to do is disable the alarm on the door to the hotel roof. Then ensure the camera in the basement car park has something obscuring its view. As an incentive, he will receive an extra five hundred pounds. And, yesterday, Dave sent one of his girls to give the man a little extra 'thank you' present.

Dave's next call is to Bekim Dardha. One of the two Albanians that Dave has used in the past. The last time was about nineteen months ago, to make something look like a hit-and-run accident.

"Bekim. I'm checking you received the payment, and that everything is all set for tomorrow night?"

"Yes. We are ready. We have the note, and we will make sure it is placed exactly as you told us. I have read what it says. It is a very clever plan." He laughs. "You are an extremely devious man, my friend."

After going over his plan one final time, Dave is happy. He rewards himself by pouring a large slug of Jack Daniel's into his whisky tumbler.

Dave puts down his drink and walks over to his shelf

unit. He carefully removes a vinyl record from its sleeve, then gently runs the anti-static cleaning cloth over the surface. He places his newly acquired copy of the Michael Garrick Sextet *Jazz Praises* LP on the turntable. He selects the first track on side two, 'Rustat's Gravesong'. The title seems kind of apt.

Dave's plan is coming together. The two Albanians are ready. His lawyer has issued a High Court claim. And Alison has told him the media is planning to run more articles against James Sheldon.

On top of this, Dave expects to become the owner of the Asbury Park estate, even if his bid is the lowest on the table. But the best part of his plan is that by tomorrow night, that 'human piece of crap' James Sheldon will be dead.

Dave raises his glass and takes a swig as the last track of the vinyl ends.

Perfect timing.

CHAPTER SEVENTY-TWO

POLICE OPERATION

Tuesday 6th December 2016

It's been two weeks since Gerry Payne reported the four men in the Fenton Motel's coffee lounge to DCI Andy Stone. He's assured him that, based on their past meetings, they'll be back today.

DCI Andy Stone is the man in charge of setting up an undercover operation. The last thing he wants to do is put anyone at risk. So the usual waitress has been given paid leave, and an undercover officer will take her place.

He has to be careful. Some criminals have the knack of spotting a trained police officer a mile away. And most female detectives are in their thirties. They need someone young and innocent-looking. So, they've brought in a newly enlisted police constable, Rachel Nason, who is in her early twenties.

They can't afford to have anything look out of place or arouse suspicion. That's why Rachel was brought into the restaurant the day before the meeting. This way, she'll have time to learn the skills she needs to play the part of a real waitress.

At 10.22 a.m., a roadside automatic number plate recognition (ANPR) camera, located close to the Fenton Motel, flags up the number plate of a silver Volvo XC90. The drug squad has tagged the vehicle as being of interest. The details are duly sent to the head of what has been named 'Operation Mandrake'.

Earlier this morning, two unmarked police vehicles parked up on the opposite side of the hotel to where Gerry had told them the suspect vehicles usually park to prevent them from being noticed by the suspects.

The other four unmarked cars are sitting in lay-bys, one pointing in the direction of London, the route they suspect the Russians will take, the other three towards Trentbridge, in a position to follow Kenny and Dave. All vehicles will be updated by PC Nason when the suspects leave the coffee lounge.

At ten thirty, four men wander in, choose a table away from other customers, and order four coffees. After the drinks have been served and the waitress is out of earshot, the Russian with better English asks if everything is okay. Receiving an affirmative answer, he stands. He gestures to the person across from him to do the same.

They make their way to the car park and open the boots of their respective vehicles. The Russians are driving a Volvo XC90, and Kenny, a black Audi A3. Both parties take out identical black briefcases. One contains a large quantity of cocaine and an unregistered pay-as-you-go mobile phone.

The other briefcase contains forty thousand pounds in cash. It also has the unregistered mobile from the previous drop.

The two men exchange briefcases, and both are locked into their respective car boots. The Russian sits in his car and sends a WhatsApp message to his colleague. It confirms the exchange has taken place and everything has gone according to plan.

Kenny drives off with the drugs hidden in the boot. Two unmarked police cars follow him, swapping places as they proceed so they won't be detected.

Five minutes later, the two men still inside the café shake hands. They look as if they are businessmen concluding a deal, which is accurate. However, the goods they are trading are highly illegal Class A drugs.

Dave pays the bill, collects the receipt and both men head out to their vehicles. Rachel goes over to clear their table, watching until they get into their respective cars.

She hurries through to the hotel kitchen and uses her police radio to update HQ. The unmarked police vehicles get the new information via the police TETRA radio system. These details are immediately passed on to DCI Andy Stone, the senior officer leading this covert operation.

Dave gets into his black Mercedes and starts the journey to meet his associate at the small secure lock-up unit he rents in Trentbridge. The Volvo with the two Russians also leaves the car park. Neither of the undercover police vehicles in the motel car park moves. They will hang back and let their colleagues sitting in a lay-by about a mile along the road take the lead. They will follow in a while. Each will take turns staying close to the target vehicles so as not to arouse suspicion.

"Delta-Six to control."

"Yes, Delta-Six."

"Confirmed sighting of Target-One. Repeat, confirmed sighting of Target-One."

The message is from one of the unmarked police vehicles following Dave's Mercedes. The two vehicles take turns, swapping places several times. Six miles later, they watch as Dave Rex drives to a block of units in a small industrial yard. The vehicles following Kenny are parked out of sight, sitting around the corner from the lock-up.

"Delta-Seven to control. Confirm Target-One at Swans Yard industrial estate on Etruria Road."

"Roger, Delta-Seven. Hold for further instructions."

The block of small units where Dave Rex and his associate are currently working is at the far end of an L-shaped yard. The unmarked police vehicles and their occupants are close by.

Four officers make their way on foot to the corner of the block of units. With the aid of small mirrors on a stick, they can peer around the corner. They can see which unit the drugs are being unloaded into.

Two police officers have been authorised to carry firearms for this operation. They remove their coats and put on flak jackets emblazoned with the word 'POLICE' in large letters. They don't anticipate any problems. But you can never tell with ruthless criminals, especially where drugs are concerned.

All four officers quietly and carefully make their way to the unit. The details of what they have seen are relayed to HQ. Everyone is in place, anxious to move in, arrest the suspects, and take charge of any items that can be used as evidence. They are just waiting for the command from DCI Stone. It comes quickly.

"Control to all units, STRIKE, STRIKE, STRIKE! I repeat, STRIKE, STRIKE, STRIKE!"

The officers move in and make their presence felt with loud cries of, "ARMED POLICE OFFICERS! PUT YOUR HANDS ABOVE YOUR HEADS!"

Dave and Kenny turn round, ready for a fight. When they see guns aimed directly at them, they comply with the command. Both men are placed in handcuffs and read their rights.

"You do not have to say anything. But it may harm your defence if you do not mention, when questioned, something which you later rely on in court. Anything you do say may be given in evidence."

"This is Delta-Six to control. Two suspects in custody. Zero shots fired. I repeat, two in custody. Zero shots fired."

"Received and understood, Delta-Six. Good work."

As he is being led away to a nearby police vehicle, Dave gulps. He will need his lawyer if he's got any chance of talking his way out of this. It looks like the recurring nightmare he's been having is about to become a reality.

CHAPTER SEVENTY-THREE

DAVE

Tuesday 6th December 2016

Following his arrest at the lock-up unit, with a large quantity of cocaine in his possession, Dave Rex is feeling as sick as a parrot.

He is currently in the main interview room at Trentbridge Police Station, being interviewed by DS Terry Underwood.

Dave is trying to protest his innocence. He's made the wise decision to have his lawyer, Mark Jackson, present. He tries putting the blame on his associate. But the detective is having none of it.

The sentence for such a large quantity of Class A drugs will see him sent down for a very long time. They also found a large quantity of cannabis at the lock-up.

"Of course, we can have a quiet word with the judge. That's if you can offer up details of your suppliers. You have to consider the people you're involved with. They might not care whether you've given us any information or not. They could decide to resolve the problem, to be on the safe side. And, right now, their biggest problem is you!"

Dave chews over the options in his mind.

The detective goes on. "Of course, if you have some juicy stuff for us, we might be able to have a word. It could be possible to get you into the Witness Protection programme."

It's a difficult option for a lot of people because they have wives and kids, but Dave only has his dear old mum. Perhaps he can take her with him.

If he sells his apartment, with the cash he has tucked away, he'll have about two and a half million pounds. The villa in Spain will need to be sold because it's in his name, and anyone looking for him will soon find it. For around fifty thousand pounds, he can have plastic surgery. If he has a hair transplant and loses some weight, it will dramatically change his appearance. No one will be able to find him. He will see to that.

The interview ends so that Dave can have a break and a quick word with his lawyer. After their meeting he'll be put back into the police cell, where he will be held while they look into his affairs.

"Dave, my secretary has informed me we received a letter this morning. It's regarding your claim over the Lotto ticket. It seems the other party has made you an offer. They say they reject your claim and say they are prepared to let the matter go to court. As they point out, that could drag on for years. Or they propose, without accepting any liability, to make an out-of-court settlement. They are offering to pay you fifty million pounds with immediate effect."

The lawyer pauses. "I'm sure you know what I'm going to say in light of your current predicament. Take what they're offering. But, of course, the final decision rests with you. I would add that they say the payment can be made within forty-eight hours."

Mark Jackson adds, "Dave, it's too late for us to reply today. So it might be wise for you to consider the offer until tomorrow. Then, if you want to go ahead, I can contact Mr Clinton Palmer, the lawyer acting for the other party, and make him aware of your decision. It means the money could be in your account by Friday."

"Yes, that seems the best thing. I'm a bit riled up and not thinking straight. I should be getting the whole amount but I'll follow your advice. After all, one day won't make much difference, will it?"

Thoughts race through Dave's head as he sits in his cell. *With fifty million, I could buy myself an island and live a life of luxury. I could travel anywhere and never have to worry about money ever again.* But in the back of his mind, the thought keeps coming back that it was *his* Lotto ticket. He deserves the whole hundred and sixty-eight million. Perhaps he should accept the offer. Then, once he is safely abroad with his new identity, he can make sure James Sheldon comes to some harm.

Usually, Dave is a clear thinker, but with all these problems, he can't seem to concentrate. He's trying to get things in order, but his mind seems like it has closed down.

What he could do with is a giant slug of Jack Daniel's. But he knows there's little chance of that.

If they offer him Witness Protection then Dave might be prepared to do a deal in exchange for giving evidence against the Russians and Mohammad. With fifty million in the bank he can buy a lot of protection. The best thing is to take his time.

He doesn't keep any incriminating evidence at his apartment. All the police have got on him are the drugs he was caught with. He's got until tomorrow to consider all his options. A thought occurs to him. Perhaps Kenny would be prepared to take the rap for everything in exchange for a couple of million.

Dave starts to relax, but something creeps into his head that causes him to shiver. He's just thought of something that's beyond his control. Something that could upset all his well-laid plans.

CHAPTER SEVENTY-FOUR

POLICE SEARCHES

Tuesday 6th December 2016

The police are anxious to search Dave Rex's apartment to see if they can find any evidence to strengthen their case. The reason for the urgency is they are worried he might have associates who could remove any potential evidence.

In charge of the search is DS Terry Underwood, assisted by PC Rachel Nason. She is still in plain clothes after working undercover as a waitress at the Fenton Motel. The pair are accompanied by two uniformed officers.

The PCs check the bedrooms and kitchen. Terry and Rachel begin in the hallway. Then they move through to the lounge and finally to Dave's office. Armed with the set of keys taken when Dave was arrested, they unlock his desk drawers. They check the filing cabinet next to his bookcase.

DS Underwood finds Dave's laptop. It doesn't have a password. Underwood checks through the files but there's not much on them. It gets put into an evidence bag. Hopefully, the tech guys will find something hidden on it.

After nearly an hour of combing the apartment, they have found nothing incriminating.

Underwood phones DCI Andy Stone with the news.

"So, you didn't find any names of associates or other addresses he might have used?"

"No, boss," Underwood admits. "The place is clean."

"That's a shame."

"Yeah. All we could find was a receipt that came in today's post. It looks like he pays for his mum's apartment just around the corner at Hanford Court Retirement Village."

"As you're in the area, I think you'd better call on her and break the news. If she reads about it in the newspaper or hears it from anyone else, it might come as a big shock. Try to break it to her gently. Don't say too much. Just tell her we're holding him for questioning at this stage."

"Righty-ho, boss."

DS Underwood and PC Nason drive to her address. Mrs Rex looks like a frail old woman and every one of her eighty years. When told the news, Mrs Rex appears to have difficulty breathing. She asks Rachel to fetch her inhaler from the bedroom.

Rachel notices it sitting on top of the cabinet on the far side of the bed. She goes to pick it up but accidentally drops the puffer on the floor. As she bends down to retrieve it, her hand brushes the storage drawer in the base of the bed. A compartment clicks open to reveal a Yale safe.

Acting on a hunch, she reaches into her bag and finds the key ring taken from Dave's possessions when he had been arrested. One of the keys has the word 'Yale' stamped on one side. She closes the compartment softly and puts the keys back into her bag. She picks up the puffer and takes it through to Mrs Rex.

Terry and Rachel wait a few minutes.

Rachel acts as if she's concerned, holding the old woman's hands.

"Are you sure you'll be all right on your own?"

"Yes, dear. I'll be fine. I have a neighbour I can call on if I need someone."

"Okay. I'll be in touch tomorrow when we know what's happening with your son. Try not to worry."

"Thank you, dear."

Once downstairs, Rachel phones DCI Andy Stone and tells him what she has discovered.

"Good work, Rachel. I'll get a warrant as soon as I can. In the meantime, keep an eye on the place."

"Okay, boss."

Andy phones the chief constable to decide on the best magistrate to approach. They need to obtain a search warrant – fast.

Two hours later, Rachel receives a call informing her the paperwork is on the way. Five minutes later, a marked police car drives into the nursing home's visitor car park. PC Nason walks over and collects an envelope containing the warrant.

"We're going back in. The DS has said you should hang around, just in case. He said to park at the back and be ready."

Rachel and DS Underwood return to the entrance and make their way towards the stairs. As they walk past the elevator, the doors open, and Mrs Rex steps out carrying four plastic carrier bags. They look full and heavy, but she is managing to carry them all.

"Hello, Mrs Rex. We were on our way to see you."

They hear the buzzer from the front entrance. DS Underwood looks at the person who has just entered. He recognises him as Eddie Collins, a known drug dealer.

When he sees the detective, he turns and starts to walk away. DS Underwood also recognises him as an associate of Dave Rex's. He radios and tells the two PCs to intercept him, search him, and take him to the police station. He will be questioned later.

Terry and Rachel get into the elevator with Mrs Rex and return to her apartment. Once inside, Rachel turns to Mrs Rex.

"We have a warrant to search these premises."

She hands it to Mrs Rex, and DS Underwood asks her for the four carrier bags.

"We're going to do an extensive search. You can save having the whole place turned upside down by telling us where to look."

"Go screw yourself. You'll get no help from me, pig," comes the reply.

CHAPTER SEVENTY-FIVE

POLICE

DS Underwood radios the PCs, asking one to come up to Mrs Rex's apartment. The other officer will take Eddie Collins to the police station. They will arrange for his vehicle to be searched later.

The PC is instructed to keep an eye on Mrs Rex while they undertake their search.

"I'll start in the bedroom," says Rachel as she walks through. She doesn't want Mrs Rex to know she noticed the safe under the bed. She has been told not to mention it. There's a chance it could be used by the defence in court and any evidence found could be thrown out on a technicality.

Rachel starts by searching the wardrobes. Then the clothes drawers until, finally, she starts to examine the bed, and pretends to see the safe for the first time.

"What have we here, Mrs Rex? There's a safe on the side of your bed base. Do you have a key for it?"

"No, I bloody don't."

"We have your son's keys. Let's see if one of these fits."

Rachel wasn't surprised when she noticed the safe.

While on holiday a few months ago, she stayed at a Premier Inn hotel. She found the king-size Hypnos bed so comfortable she decided to buy one.

When she visited a local shop to see if they sold them, the salesman showed her the bed. He also pointed out the optional extra. For three hundred and fifty pounds, he told her, she could have a built-in safe in the bed base.

"A lot of people use it for laptops, and things like their passports," he told her.

She ended up buying the bed, but without the optional extra.

Rachel opens the safe and discovers it's empty. Moving back into the lounge, she whispers to her colleague.

He looks at Mrs Rex. "Can you tell me what I'll find in these carrier bags, Mrs Rex?"

"I don't know. Some things I found and was about to throw out. It's only rubbish."

The DS removes the contents of one of the bags and lays the items across the coffee table.

After examining them, he phones DCI Stone and puts him on speakerphone.

"Hello, boss. We've found several items we think will be of interest. We'll pack everything up here and be back at the station shortly."

He ends the call. "It looks like we underestimated you, Mrs Rex. We took you for a frail old lady, but the truth is you're still razor-sharp. You had an idea we'd come back, didn't you? So you called one of your son's associates to come and collect all the incriminating evidence. Luckily, we managed to get a warrant in time.

"We saw him downstairs as he was about to come in. I don't think your son will be visiting you in the future.

Where he's going, it's far more likely you'll have to visit *him*."

All the items from the carrier bags are bagged up. Everything will be taken back to the station for closer inspection.

The officers are standing by the front door and about to leave. Terry turns to Dave's mum. He smiles sweetly. "I can honestly say it's been a real pleasure, Mrs Rex."

She doesn't reply – but if looks could kill!

The PC, Terry and Rachel go down to their car and head back to Trentbridge Police Station.

They head for the incident room, where the contents of their haul are laid out on the tables. The detectives put on disposable gloves to examine the items in more detail. As they go through each item, it's labelled and catalogued.

DCI Andy Stone gasps when he views the spread of items. He turns to DS Underwood and PC Nason. "Wow. What you've found is a treasure trove of information. It's a rare find – an insight into the workings of a master criminal. Congratulations to both of you."

Andy looks at the list from the evidence log, then picks up the first of two black notebooks. This one is marked 'Transfers'.

"Well, well. What have we here?" It contains what appears to be the accounts for Dave's legit companies. It also shows how much cash he's been putting in from his drug business. Then he goes to the second notebook, marked 'Girls'.

"This is a surprise." The second notebook gives details of Rex's escort agency, the business offering the services of Eastern European call girls.

"Bloody hell," says Andy, "look at this."

They all stare at the manila document file marked 'Lotto'.

Reading the notes shows Dave has taken court action against James Sheldon. In the court papers, Dave alleges that James cheated him out of the winning ticket.

They find a note that seems to prove a gentleman by the name of Tim Knox has received two thousand pounds. It shows he's been paid to lie and say he was there when Dave purchased the winning Lotto ticket.

Another file has photos of men caught in compromising positions with young women. Each photo has a man's name written on the back – fourteen men in total. They recognise one as a local politician and another as a high-ranking police officer way above their pay grades. They assume the men are unaware they have been captured on film. There are four photos with the name Peter Hogan.

They find detailed plans of where James Sheldon lives and his car registration. It also includes what appears to be a draft copy of a suicide note. It's filed with another piece of paper that shows repeated attempts to copy James Sheldon's signature.

They find details of the porter at the Grand Hotel and a note that shows monies paid to him every week.

Another file contains information relating to a Russian drugs supplier. There are also details of a man who appears to supply Dave with cannabis. There is a mobile phone with a note attached by a rubber band. It reads, 'Phone to arrange next meeting.'

Terry Underwood is pretty sure it will be an unregistered phone, untraceable, but it's worth calling the one number stored on it. He dials it. A voice that sounds Russian answers.

"Hello," DS Underwood says, "Dave Rex is ill. He's asked me to arrange the next meeting."

The man hangs up.

CHAPTER SEVENTY-SIX

DAVE

Tuesday 6th December 2016

At eight thirty-five p.m., DS Underwood walks down to Dave Rex's cell, accompanied by the custody officer, who unlocks the door.

"Dave. I thought you'd like to know. We obtained a search warrant for your mum's apartment and found the contents of your safe. As you can imagine, we've discovered a mountain of evidence regarding your activities. My, my, you have been a busy boy, haven't you.

"We'll be interviewing you again tomorrow morning, and I think you'll have a lot of new questions to answer. I'll contact your lawyer and let him know.

"My team and I are calling it a day. We're off down the pub for a well-deserved pint or two. Sadly, you won't be able to join us." He gives Dave a broad smile. The custody officer closes the cell door.

DS Underwood calls Mark Jackson and leaves a message on his voicemail. He tells him about the search and gives some indication of the evidence they've found, adding that they will be interviewing his client at ten a.m. sharp the following morning.

By eight forty-five p.m., most of the detectives working the case are sitting in the Sutherland Arms, having a well-deserved pint.

At nine p.m., Dave's lawyer arrives at the police station and explains he needs to see his client. It is a matter of extreme urgency.

The front desk operative is a civilian rather than a police officer. Another casualty of budget cuts. He phones the custody sergeant, Owen Franks, and explains the situation. He agrees to arrange for the pair to meet in Interview Room 3. He passes instructions to the duty officer to bring Dave up from his cell.

The sergeant goes out to reception and opens the security door to allow the lawyer access. He leads him along the corridor to the interview room.

After two minutes, a uniformed officer appears with Dave.

"I need to speak with my client on a private matter."

Both officers leave the room. After a further two minutes, there's a loud noise and shouting from inside the interview room. Someone is frantically banging on the door.

"Officers, come quickly. I think my client's having a heart attack. Please hurry."

Owen Franks rushes in, crouches down next to the man and checks to see if there is a pulse or even a hint of breath. He detects neither.

The uniformed officer takes out his police phone and calls for an ambulance. He then goes to assist his colleague who is attempting resuscitation.

Eight minutes later, the ambulance arrives. Dave is stretchered out of the rear entrance of the police station. A police officer accompanies Dave to the ambulance. The vehicle speeds off with its blue lights flashing.

Meanwhile, after a brief chat with the officers, the lawyer leaves via the front entrance. He walks outside and dials a number on his mobile.

"Da."

The lawyer speaks with his more pronounced natural accent, "*Sdelano*" (Done).

He takes the SIM card from the phone, breaks it in half and throws it into a nearby rubbish bin.

Inside A&E at Trentbridge Hospital, a nurse stands on one side of an examination table, looking over at the exhausted doctor.

"You've done everything you can. I'll write it up. I just need you to say it."

The doctor takes a deep breath and then looks directly at the nurse, his face resigned to the situation.

"I pronounce this patient deceased." He glances at his watch. "The time is 9.44 p.m."

The following morning, Dave's lawyer turns up at the time stated on his voicemail message.

"Dead? I don't understand. What happened?"

"But you were here last night when he collapsed."

"I certainly was not. Who told you that?"

"The night-time duty sergeant."

"I can assure you, Detective, that I certainly did not visit the police station last night. I was at the theatre with my wife all evening."

CHAPTER SEVENTY-SEVEN

SUICIDE

Wednesday 7th December 2016

There's a knock on the door of the office of MJA Housing Foundation, and two men walk in. One is around thirty years old, dressed in a smart suit with an air of authority about him. The other is in uniform. His fresh-faced appearance seems to confirm police officers are getting younger.

"I'm looking for Susan Hartman," says the man in the suit.

"That's me," Susan replies.

"Hello, I'm Detective Sergeant Howard Neave." He produces a warrant card and holds it up for Susan to see.

"Do you know a Mr James Sheldon?"

"Yes. He's the founder of this charity. He's not here at the moment. Is there a problem?"

"I'm afraid you need to prepare yourself for some bad news. At eight o'clock last night we received a call from the Grand Hotel. It appears that a man we believe to be Mr James Sheldon jumped from their roof."

"No! It can't be." Susan slumps onto her chair. "Are you sure it's James?"

"We believe so. There was a suicide note in his pocket, which is how we found you. As we understand it, he has no immediate family. We wondered if someone who knows him would be prepared to come and identify the body. I must warn you that he fell from a great height and sustained major facial injuries. It won't be an easy task. He's a former police officer, so we're currently checking his fingerprints. We'll have confirmation at some point this afternoon. But we do need a formal identification."

"I... I see. Well, yes, I suppose I should be the person to do that."

"If we come back to collect you at around two o'clock, we'll be happy to give you a lift and then bring you back. In the meantime, I wonder if you can help us in another way. As I mentioned, he left a suicide note." The detective shows her a picture on his iPad.

> 'I'm so sorry for everything I 've done. Now the truth has come out, you will have realised I stole the Lotto ticket and the idea for Asbury Park. I will have to give back the money. I wanted to be rich. Without the money, life is not worth living. I don't want to face everyone. I have decided this is the best way out. Please forgive me.
>
> *James'*

Susan Hartman looks up at the detective. "That's not a

note written by the man I've come to know. I don't believe it. I don't believe a word of it."

CHAPTER SEVENTY-EIGHT

JAMES

Wednesday 7th December 2016

After an early night, my migraine has finally gone. It's ten thirty. I walk past the main entrance desk of our office building, wondering why the receptionist is looking at me in such a strange way. I go up to the first floor and enter MJA Housing Foundation's general office.

"Good morning, everyone," I say in a cheerful voice.

Susan, Fiona, and Alison are seated together. It looks as if Susan and Fiona have been crying.

"Is there a problem I should know about?" I enquire.

Susan jumps up, looking shocked. "James! You're alive!"

"Eh? Yes. I know I looked like death warmed up yesterday, but I feel much better now."

"No, I mean, we had the police here first thing this morning. They told us you were dead. They said you jumped off a building. That you committed suicide."

"I'm not sure what's going on, but as you can see, I'm

here and very much alive. It must be some sort of mistake. Why did they think it was me?"

CHAPTER SEVENTY-NINE

THE PREVIOUS EVENING - TUESDAY 6TH DECEMBER 2016

After arriving home at Meadowcroft, James takes two paracetamol tablets. He heads straight to his bedroom to sleep off his migraine.

Stevie has arranged to go out with Jackie Houston, a girl he's recently met who works in the Mayflower coffee shop in the centre of town. He's meeting her outside Henry's Bar on Quayside at eight o'clock.

At seven thirty, having had a shower and changed into clean clothes, Stevie looks out of the window. It's raining.

He doesn't want to disturb James. But that's not a problem. James has said he can borrow the car any time.

The nearest car park to Henry's Bar is at least a three-minute walk. He sees James's thick winter overcoat in the hall, and, after a moment's thought, Stevie picks it up and throws it on. He knows James won't mind.

He gently closes the front door and walks down to the car park, pulling up the collar of the coat to shield himself from the wind and rain. He dashes to the car with his head down inside the coat.

He's barely had time to shut the driver's door and put the key in the ignition when the passenger door opens, and a large figure jumps in beside him. For a moment, he thinks it's James, recovered from his migraine. However, when he sees the gun pointed at his side, Stevie freezes.

"What do you want? I've only got fifty pounds in cash. It's yours."

"I don't want your money. Drive where I tell you," states a voice with a heavy Southern European accent.

Stevie is given instructions as he drives.

After ten minutes, the passenger snaps. "Pull into the car park. Stop at the far end and then get out of the car."

The gunman slips his free hand into his left pocket as he keeps his weapon trained on Stevie. He doesn't take his eyes away or lower the gun for a second.

"Stand against the wall," he commands.

He pulls out his phone and calls a number.

"We're here. Come down."

The lift opens, and out steps another heavily built man. He makes his way over.

"Turn round," he barks as he ties Stevie's hands behind his back.

"What's going on? I thought this was a robbery. Don't you want my money? What's this all about?"

"Silence, or you'll get it," says the first man.

They wait as the second man calls the lift. When it arrives, all three get in.

When the doors re-open, the second man looks both ways along the hallway, then beckons them to follow. They turn right and walk to a door at the end marked 'Emergency Exit'.

The door is opened, and Stevie is pushed out into a cold

wind driving across the building's roof. The second man reaches into his jacket pocket and produces a piece of paper. He looks at it, keeping it in his gloved hand. He seems to be reading it. Then he gives out a short chuckle. He folds the paper and puts it into Stevie's left-hand coat pocket.

Stevie gives the man a quizzical look. "What do you want from me? What have I done to you? What's this all about?"

The man holding Stevie's tied hands pushes him forward.

Stevie is panicking. He feels a small leak of pee in his pants. He is shaking. He knows it's more from fear than the cold.

All he knows is, at this point, he would gladly tell them anything.

Suddenly, and to Stevie's relief, the first man unties his hands. It looks like they are going to let him go. They must have realised this was some sort of mistake. In a second, he'll be free.

With his hands released, Stevie opens his mouth. "Please, tell me what the hell's going on?"

The first man lifts his hands and gives Stevie a massive push. As he falls backwards, he trips over something.

That something is the edge of the building.

CHAPTER EIGHTY

JAMES

Thursday 8th December 2016

Tell me, God, what have I done to deserve this? I must be King Midas in reverse. Everything I touch turns to death. First, it was my wife and kids, and now my lovely friend Stevie.

Susan has tried to help, just like my friends did after the hit-and-run, but I want to be on my own. I've told her I'll be back in a few days. I've driven up to North Wales, to a place close to Snowdonia, where Miriam and I once went on holiday. A lovely remote hotel called Plas Maenan. I can hide away here and shut out the world. No TV, no newspapers, and no awkward questions. I didn't even bring my mobile.

It's also a few miles past Rhyl, Stevie's hometown. Once I've plucked up the courage, I'll go and see his family to talk about the funeral arrangements. I'll make sure it's nothing but the best.

A couple of days ago, Stevie and I were looking forward to helping hundreds of families start a new life. Now I'm mourning the loss of my dear friend. I've got no idea what's going on back at the charity's offices, and, for the next day or two, I really don't care.

The only reason I'm going ahead with our plans is because I know it's what Stevie would have wanted. Since he became involved with the charity, his ideas and enthusiasm helped to transform it from an idea into a reality. Everyone has become so much more fired up about what we're doing. I can't let him down.

I need a couple of days on my own to grieve, to remember the friendship he extended me when I needed it most. I need to cherish his memory and find the strength to carry on.

God bless you, Stevie. I'll do everything I can to make you proud.

CHAPTER EIGHTY-ONE

THE TRUTH IS REVEALED

Thursday 8th December 2016

Local social media is on fire. The *Trentbridge Times* is disappearing from the newsagents' shelves. Copies are flying out faster than anyone can remember in its entire hundred-and-twenty-eight-year history.

It leads with the headline:

'Lotto Winner Cleared of Cheating'

With the sub-heading:

'Suspected Drug Lord Dies in Police Custody'

The front-page story reads:

> A local businessman at the centre of a controversy over the alleged theft of a winning lottery ticket has died in police custody. Police had arrested the man earlier in the day at a small unit on Etruria Road, on suspicion of large-scale drug dealing. He and another man were found to be in possession of cocaine with a

street value of two hundred and eighty thousand pounds.

David Rex, aged fifty, of Brampton Manor, Trentbridge, died of a suspected heart attack. Officers say he was in an interview room with a person believed to be his lawyer when he collapsed. Mr Rex was treated by paramedics at the police station. He was then taken to Trentbridge Hospital, where he was pronounced dead just before ten p.m.

Mr Rex had recently claimed that the hundred and sixty-eight-million-pound winning Lotto ticket holder, James Sheldon, had stolen his ticket. He also accused him of stealing plans to redevelop the Asbury Park estate for the benefit of the community.

When police searched a local address, they found evidence that the story of the stolen Lotto ticket was false. They also confirmed the plans were those proposed by Mr Sheldon via a charity he set up called the MJA Housing Foundation.

Police believe that Mr Rex is also behind a recent murder that was staged to look like a suicide.

An inquest into the death of Mr Rex will be held at Trentbridge Coroner's Court following a post-mortem.'

Buried away on page seven of the same newspaper is a much smaller article:

'The Albion Hotel, recently earmarked for redevelopment, has been purchased. The buyer intends to

> continue running it as a hotel. It is expected to remain open throughout the period of renovation and refurbishment. This is good news, as no jobs will be lost, and it is anticipated extra staff will be taken on in due course.'

The planning committee is relieved to hear the news about Dave Rex. This means that when they cast their vote, they can accept the highest bid. It means the council will receive a much better deal.

It also means the Asbury Park project can go ahead and enhance the town of Trentbridge. Now that the highest bidder has been exonerated, this will make them look good.

CHAPTER EIGHTY-TWO

PETER HOGAN

Thursday 8th December 2016

Peter Hogan sits at his office desk reading the front-page story of the local newspaper. He realises the two-hundred-and-fifty-thousand-pound pay-off he has been expecting from Dave Rex is not going to materialise. That means his plans to leave his wife and move in with Monique will have to be put on hold.

As he sits, wondering what to do, his secretary pops her head around the door.

"Peter. There's someone on the phone for you. I asked his name and what it was about, but all he said was, 'Tell Peter it's Mr H.' Do you want to take it?"

"Yes, Cynthia, put him through."

"Hello, Harry. Why the cloak and dagger?"

"I thought I'd give you a word of warning. You're in deep shit. You can expect a visit from Mr Plod any day."

Peter shivers at the thought. "How do you know that?"

"I have a contact on the inside. I just want to make

sure that when they do come knocking, you don't have anything that ties me to any of our, shall we say, *private deals*."

"No, Harry. I assure you. I've kept nothing."

"That's good to hear. Just so you know, Peter. Your mistress has left. She didn't hang around. If I were you, I'd find someone to take care of your, shall we say, *desires*, while you have the chance because where you're going, there won't be any women."

"You... You really think they'll send me to prison?"

"Oh yes, Peter. No doubt about that. I called to let you know that as we go back a few years, while you're away, I'll keep an eye on your wife and make sure she's financially taken care of."

Peter shivers again at the thought. "Er, thank you, Harry. That's much appreciated."

"Well Peter, I guess the next time I see you will be in a few years when you get out. Good luck."

With that, the phone line goes dead.

Three days later, Peter is sitting in his office. He's spent the last hour shuffling pieces of paper around but not actually getting anything done.

Cynthia knocks at his door.

"Er, Peter. There are three police officers here. They say they need to have a word with you."

"Yes. I've been expecting them. Please send them in."

DS Underwood walks in, followed by two police officers.

"Good morning," says the detective. "Peter Hogan. We are here to arrest you. I will read you your rights, and then we'll take you to the police station. We have several questions we'd like you to answer."

The police have been to the offices of the MJA Housing Foundation and taken Alison Crook into custody. A search of her house has found just over nine thousand pounds in cash. This has been seized under the *Proceeds of Crime Act.*

CHAPTER EIGHTY-THREE

POLICE RAIDS

Friday 9th December 2016

The drug squad at Trentbridge police is working overtime. The information gleaned from Dave Rex's notebooks and files at his mum's apartment has revealed a list of local drug dealers. The scale of information is so large that extra officers have had to be drafted in from neighbouring forces to help handle the planned raids on the various individuals' homes.

It seems Dave kept extremely detailed notes with names, addresses, mobile phone numbers and details of what they bought and when. With court orders, the police can gather evidence against all these dealers that will stand up in any court of law.

And following the death of Dave Rex, it appears his accomplice, Kenny Green, has agreed to give evidence in the hope of getting a shorter sentence.

The drug squad decides to strike before all the dealers realise their details have been found in Dave's notebooks.

Three days after sifting through all the information,

there are coordinated raids on twenty-two separate addresses at five in the morning, and a total of twenty-six people are arrested on suspicion of being involved in the supply of illegal drugs.

Amongst those arrested are:

Sniffy McFee is so stoned he thinks the large bangs he heard are thunder and the torch beams are lightning. However it's the sound of a steel-constructed police enforcer being pounded against his front door, followed by armed police with flashlights.

He sits up from the mattress on the floor of his grotty one-room bedsit, as a police officer handcuffs him. The room is so small it only takes two minutes to find his stash of suspected illegal drugs.

When police raid the home of thirty-four-year-old Nina Crickshaw, they find cocaine with a street value of thirty-two thousand pounds hidden in a kitchen cupboard alongside papers from a court appearance, just the day before, when she was given a suspended sentence for supplying drugs. Officers also find drug paraphernalia and her mobile phone, containing messages that indicate she's been dealing.

After smashing their way into the home of thirty-year-old Abdul Zafeer and clearly shouting "ARMED POLICE", two officers find themselves facing a man brandishing a two-foot-long machete and screaming, "Come anywhere near me and I'll cut yer fucking heads off!" Despite pleas for him to drop the weapon, he lunges forward and one officer is left with no alternative other than to use PAVA spray to blind the attacker. He is then disarmed, wrestled to the ground and handcuffed.

A search reveals packages of heroin and a large quantity of cocaine with a combined street value of thirty-eight thousand pounds hidden in an upstairs bedroom. Officers also find dealers' bags, cling film, cutting agents, plastic gloves, two sets of digital scales, two lock knives and £12,400 in cash.

Three miles away in Trumpington, a far more respectable area of town, the same thing is happening at the four-bedroom home of Chashida Masood, who thought he had been clever by burying the drugs in his back garden. It takes the sniffer dog less than five minutes to tell his handler where to dig. They find cocaine, heroin and cannabis with a street value of eighty-five thousand pounds.

Some of the people arrested are transferred to other police stations because Trentbridge only has twelve cells and, due to the serious nature of the offences, it's not possible to have more than one person in each cell.

It's by far the largest drugs operation Trentbridge police have ever been involved in.

Of course, within days of them putting these dealers away, others will take their place. But that's the name of the game. However, the convictions will do wonders for arrest targets. And it's rumoured that a few commendations might be in the offing.

CHAPTER EIGHTY-FOUR

JAMES

January 2017

I'm not sure how many people ever get the chance to write out a cheque for over thirty-five million pounds. But that's exactly what I did yesterday.

I was sitting in the hallowed chambers of the Trentbridge Council members' boardroom. I had my lawyer by my side. I handed the council chairman the cheque. In return, I received the deeds confirming the charity I've set up is now the owner of the entire Asbury Park estate.

After the ceremony, we were escorted into a smaller room for the announcement to be made to the waiting media scrum.

The first thing we had to do was say 'cheese' for all the photographers. It seems local politicians want to make sure they get their pictures in the media. Especially as it's coming up to election time.

Then I spent nearly twenty minutes answering questions from journalists. Susan and Fiona handed out media packs.

Yesterday evening, we appeared on the local TV news as the top story.

Today, we're front-page news in the *Trentbridge Times*. I remember the article they ran when I won the hundred and sixty-eight million. I sit to see how many facts they get right this time:

Local Lotto winner James Sheldon has handed over a cheque for more than thirty-five million pounds to the council. His charity is now the owner of the Asbury Park estate.

Mr Sheldon told this newspaper he expects work to start on refurbishing the houses in the next few days.

He hopes an initial two hundred houses will be ready for occupancy within the next twelve months. Followed by a further six hundred and eighty houses over the following year or two.

Two firms of local builders have been contracted to undertake the work. They have been chosen on their reputation for high-quality workmanship.

He has also confirmed that once the council have approved the plans, work will start on restoring the bridge across the River Stern. This will connect Asbury Park directly with the town. The cost is estimated at forty million pounds.

When asked about paying out so much money, Mr Sheldon replied:

"Luckily, I can afford it. I haven't spent much from the money I won. I bought a second-hand Ford Mondeo and a three-bedroom house. I've been a bit of a miser. So if you're expecting me to say I've got a yacht and a private jet on order, then I'm afraid you're going to be disappointed. I aim to keep giving money to local worthy causes."

Before he won the Lotto, Mr Sheldon spent ten months homeless and on the streets. He says his priority is to help families who deserve a better start in life. People should expect to have a decent way of living without worrying if they can afford the rent. Everyone should have a roof over their heads.

The joint head of the charity, Susan Hartman, has volunteered with various local charities for over twelve years. She has compiled a list of sixty families she considers will be good tenants. They will all be invited to see the first set of refurbished houses then asked for their views on what they would like and how the properties should be decorated.

The houses were originally built by the council in the late 1970s to a high standard. Each has its own garden and garage.

Mr Sheldon said the rent for a three-bedroom house will be three hundred pounds a month. Most families currently living in private rented properties, many of which are small flats with no garden, pay between six and eight hundred.

The charity has contracted the council workforce to repair all the roads around the site.

He went on to say that his charity is in talks with a major chain for a supermarket to be built. This will be alongside a school, a doctors' surgery, and a pharmacy.

It is expected this will bring hundreds of jobs into the local economy.

EPILOGUE

June 2017

We have arranged for a grand opening ceremony. This is to mark the first sixty families moving in. The bridge construction has also been completed.

Of course, all the local officials are coming to the opening for the free food, drink and publicity. Even the Secretary of State for Transport is coming up from London.

I've received approval for three of the streets to be renamed. So, I invited Miriam's parents to come and see the estate. I was happy they gave me their blessing when they saw the three roads named after their beloved daughter and grandchildren.

Miriam Close, Jack Close and Abigail Close. And the new bridge road is to be called Stevie's Way.

Work on the school was finalised two weeks ago. The doctors' surgery is complete and should be open within four weeks. An adjoining pharmacy has been added to the original plans.

BT kept its promise, so the entire area now has broadband. A 4G mobile phone mast has been installed, so everyone can receive a good signal. Many businesses have shown an interest in the facilities.

Over the coming year, it's hoped another two hundred families will be able to move in.

Susan is training our office manager, Fiona Dean, to take over the running of the charity when Susan retires. She will continue to be involved, but on a part-time basis.

I'm looking forward to seeing more families move in and watching the area coming back to life, just as Susan and I planned, along with Stevie's help. I still miss him.

The opening ceremony turned out to be the biggest event in Trentbridge for many years. I invited the staff from the Albion Hotel, and they all turned up.

As to what's next in my life, I have no idea. All I know is... giving away money to deserving causes gives me a great deal of pleasure. It's something I intend to go on doing until the money runs out.

I've still got the Ford Mondeo, and I've moved into the house at 27 Foundry Road.

I bumped into Martin Hammond recently. He told me he and his wife are expecting a baby. They still live in Primrose Square.

I've also bumped into Julia from Coverdale's Estate Agents, who looks as stunning as ever, but only to say hello. I don't think I'll ever love anyone but my beautiful Miriam.

Whenever I want to feel close to her, I go onto YouTube and search for 'When I Call' by Ghost Dance. We heard it at a disco at university and it became our song: three minutes and thirty seconds of pure joy, and a tune as beautiful as her. Listening to the haunting melody brings her back to me.

But there *could* be a new lady in my life soon. I went to Birmingham the other day and popped into the Ferrari car showroom and saw a brand new 488GTB. She's a beauty, and I just might bring her home to live with me!

I know there's no chance of getting reinstated into the police force. So I've been talking to my friend and ex-colleague Phil Jones. We've discussed the possibility of me buying into his private investigator business and becoming a partner.

I walked along Market Street and past Tindall's Convenience Store yesterday. One thing I'm sure of, I won't be buying another Lotto ticket. But it shouldn't stop *you* trying.

Who knows?

You could become the next Mr or Mrs Lucky.

Thank you for reading Mr Lucky. I hope you enjoyed it.

In the next book of the series, Lucky Break, there's a murder at the Albion Hotel. Pit your wits against the top detectives of Trentbridge police and see if you can spot the killer. Over the page you can read chapter one.

Lucky Break - Chapter One

Harold Croft had come to Trentbridge Auctions hoping to win *Lot 178*, which the catalogue described as a job lot of professional decorating tools and equipment in excellent condition.

He desperately needed them for the contract from Orchid Construction to decorate sixteen apartments. He'd got the work for one reason and one reason only—the price. What they were paying him was daylight robbery. He knew Orchid was charging the site developers the top rate, but he was in no position to argue. It was the first work he'd been offered in three months.

Once he started the work next week, he'd get an advance payment that would just about keep his head above water. It was money he desperately needed if he was going to catch up with the four mortgage payments he'd missed.

According to the catalogue, the lot had an estimated two hundred pounds sale price. Luckily, he still had one credit card that wasn't maxed out. But to be on the safe side, he checked the balance on his phone—six hundred and twenty pounds before he reached his limit.

He glanced impatiently at his watch. It would be at least

an hour before the tools went under the hammer. To kill some time, he might as well have a wander around.

As Harold rummaged through the box labelled 'Property of Burlington House'. As he pulled out a rolled-up canvas painting, a piece of paper dropped to the floor. He stooped down to pick it up.

The letter had the crest of Sotheby's Auction House of London. It was clearly old. Harold could tell because of the dried brown stains and the impressions left by the keys of a typewriter. The date at the top of the letter confirmed it was from a decade before the invention of computers and desktop printers: July 7th, 1963.

Harold could feel his palms sweating and butterflies forming in his stomach as he read each line. He glanced around to ensure no one was watching. Then, as inconspicuously as possible, he placed the letter into his pocket. He couldn't risk anyone else being able to read the contents.

He wandered over to a quiet corner of the room. He had to be absolutely sure this was genuine. He took out the note and reread it. There was no doubt. The painting was worth a fortune.

The letter from Sotheby's was addressed to Lord Cunningham, Burlington House, Old Priory Lane, Buckshott. It read:

7th July 1963

Dear Lord Cunningham,

Thank you for allowing our expert to visit your lovely home and examine the painting of the lady in the pink dress. I am delighted to confirm it is indeed an original work by the artist Giovanni Boldini.

The subject of the painting is an actress and socialite, Marthe de Florian. A lady famed for her captivating beauty. Our research shows it was completed in 1898 in Paris when she was 24 years old. It is regarded as a work of significant importance. It is, therefore, of considerable value. Recently, similar works have sold for upwards of seven figures.

I understand you are not looking to sell at the moment. However, should the opportunity arise at some point in the future, I can assure you that our auction house would be able to obtain the very highest price. We have a unique and exclusive list of buyers from around the world.

Yours sincerely,

Anton De-Bonneville

It hadn't been Harold's intention to bid on a box of what, at first, looked like worthless junk. But now he could see it included a genuine masterpiece. As he hung around waiting, he had a second stroke of luck.

He noticed a man wearing a tweed hunting jacket with elbow patches. His eyeglasses perched on the bridge of his nose. With an air of great authority, the man stepped forward and began to examine the box's contents. Harold manoeuvred his way around until he was standing unseen behind the man. He moved a little closer as the man took out his mobile and made a call. Harold didn't hear all of the conversation, but he heard enough.

"Yes, it's in a box from Burlington House. I remember seeing the painting hanging in the library years ago. The old bugger must have passed away. It looks like it's been accidentally dumped in with a box of old tat. The estimate says ten to twenty pounds. I hope nobody else has seen it. It's worth a bloody fortune. I can afford to bid up to five hundred pounds, but that's my limit."

Harold knew this was his once-in-a-lifetime opportunity.

"And now, ladies and gentlemen, we come to Lot 92—a box containing miscellaneous items from the property of Burlington Country House. Let's start the bidding at twenty pounds. Do I hear twenty?"

"I have twenty. Do I hear twenty-two, twenty-five, thirty now? Any advance on thirty?"

Harold noticed the rival bidder standing a few feet in front. He was looking around, trying to see who else was bidding.

Three minutes later, the man raised his hand with a bid of five hundred pounds.

"Any advance on five hundred? Do I hear five hundred and twenty?"

The room remained silent.

Harold watched the man's posture change, assuming he had placed what would be the winning bid.

The auctioneer's eyes swept around the room.

"If you're all done?

"Going once, going twice..."

Harold grinned and raised his hand.

Be sure to grab your copy of Lucky Break, to find out what happens next.

A MASTERPIECE FOUND IN A JUNK SHOP
LEADS TO MURDER A GROWING LIST OF SUSPECTS
BUT TIME IS RUNNING OUT
ALL THE POLICE NEED IS ONE LUCKY BREAK
LUCKY BREAK
BRITISH CRIME THRILLER - BOOK 2
LEE WOOD

About The Author

My name is Lee Wood, and I write British Crime Thrillers that take you on a rollercoaster ride.

I've always been interested in crime and started reading *Sherlock Holmes* when I was about eight years old.

I even helped the police solve a crime when I was only eleven years old after buying several books on what today would be called forensics.

Apart from writing and reading books, my other passion is music.

I live in Cambridge with my lovely wife, Elizabeth.

You can stay in touch with me via my website
https://leewoodauthor.com

BRITISH CRIME WRITER

Would you consider leaving a review?

If you enjoyed this book, it would be wonderful if you could leave a review on Amazon to tell other readers.

Reviews are the best way for other people to discover this book. A few words will do, although if you want to say more, that would be fine.

Thank you

I really enjoy what my readers think about my books. I read every message, so if you want to, send a link to your review, send me a photo or tell me a little about yourself. Whatever you have to say, I'd love to hear from you.

You can get in touch with me via
leewoodauthor@gmail.com
or
www.facebook.com/leewoodauthor

About The Trentbridge Crime Series

What's it all about?
There are currently seven books in this series. You can read them in ANY order. Each book is a standalone story, so there are no cliffhangers at the end of the book. However, some themes run between each book.
If you have only read one or two books, I hope you will consider checking out the entire series.
Each book is set in the fictional town of Trentbridge, which is actually based on Stoke-on-Trent.
There are various characters for you to follow. These include James Sheldon, who was a detective sergeant until his family were killed. Then we have Detective Inspector Eden Gold, Detective Sergeant Tracy Archer and DS Carla Parsons.

A crime series that doesn't play by the rules
With most crime series, you know that whatever happens, it usually ends with the good guys winning the day. With this series of books, that's not always the case. The idea is to bring you stories with more twists and turns than a rollercoaster.

I love hearing from my readers.
You can connect with me either on Facebook or via my website, www.leewoodauthor.com
I ALWAYS reply to messages as I love hearing from readers.

I am currently looking for ARC readers. You receive an advance copy of the book in return for checking the book and letting me know about any mistakes or plot holes you find.
If that seems of interest, please check out my website for more details.

Thank you. Lee

Printed in Dunstable, United Kingdom

64045567R00181